Death Angel

David Tylor

Death Angel

ISBN 978-1-7782474-5-3

9 781778 247453

Carol

I cannot love you anymore than I do,

You completely consume me,

I am absolutely, madly in love with you,

You and me Forever

Dave

In the long, sleepless watches of the night,
  A gentle face — the face of one long dead —
  Looks at me from the wall, where round its head
  The night-lamp casts a halo of pale light.

The Cross of Snow, H.W. Longfellow
1807 - 1882

Chapter 1

Dr. Marianne Bevan, County Medical Examiner, sat in her cramped office surrounded by the things she loved. When the new Police Services Building was being built, she had been offered a whole wing of the building to do with what she pleased. But, in spite of the urgings by just about everyone on her staff, she had turned the offer down. She felt comfortable staying in her existing office surrounded with her 20 plus years of memories. And, considering her dislike for driving, being close to the Regional Morgue was an added bonus.

This morning, when she had left her condo on her way to work, she had forgotten to take her umbrella with her and ended up being caught in a surprise early downpour. Now, with her hair still wet, she had her head buried in a stack of papers that were spread out across her desk. As part of her weekly routine, she always reviewed the recently released Mortality Reports that were issued by each of the county's four hospitals. Today, she was puzzled. Something didn't look quite right to her trained eye. Her normal, mundane review of the mortality numbers from the hospitals showed an abnormality. She checked, double checked, then checked again. There was no mistaking it, it was there. The number of sudden deaths reported by St. Luke's Memorial Hospital had taken a noticeable jump. When she compared the numbers against the numbers reported by the other three area hospitals, the increase was alarming. She cross checked the numbers from St. Luke's against the weekly activity report issued by the CDC. The Center for Disease Control made no mention of any 'Hot Spot' activity in the service area of the hospital. She then scoured through her computer in a search of the various government web sites. The FBI, the Department of Transportation, the State Police and none made any mention of any significant event that would have caused such a rapid rise in the number of reported deaths. This abnormality was solely contained within the walls of St. Luke's Memorial Hospital.

"Marjorie," she called out to her assistant. "Can you see if Jason is in his office. Tell him I'd like to see him, please."

Within minutes there was a brief knock on her door as her Senior Medical Investigator, Jason Adler, walked into her office. As he stood before her, clean, dry, as if rain would never dare to fall on him, Marianne couldn't help herself. Whenever she looked at her investigator, she wished she was twenty years younger. He was tall, well built with not an ounce of fat on his muscular body. His reddish-brown hair had just the right amount of wildness to it that it gave his face the look of adventure. And when he looked at her with his steely blue eyes that could melt ice at thirty paces, she always ended up holding her breath.

“You wanted to see me?”

At the sound of his voice, she snapped back to reality. “Yes,” she answered. “Have you had a chance to look at this week’s Mortality Reports?”

“I had a quick look at them,” he said. “Why? I didn’t notice anything unusual.”

“You didn’t?” she asked in a surprised voice. It took her a moment to remind herself that she really shouldn’t be surprised that it had slipped past Jason. He didn’t have near the amount of experience she had absorbed through her years on the job.

“I think you’d better look at them again,” she stated. “When I look at them, I’m pretty sure the numbers lead me to believe there’s an active serial killer operating out of St. Luke’s Memorial Hospital.”

“Whoa! Whoa!” Jason called out in alarm as he waved his hands in front of her. “Those are some pretty heavy words to be throwing around.” He knew Doctor Bevan to be a very conscientious Medical Examiner who took her work seriously. If something in the report alarmed her, then he wanted to know about it. “What proof do you have to be making such a claim?”

"It's all here in the numbers," Marianne replied as she pointed her finger at the papers on her desk.

"Show me," Jason said as he leaned over the doctor's desk, bringing his head closer to hers. As Marianne pointed out the numbers of concern that were hidden in the report, the musky scent from his aftershave caused her toes to silently curl inside her shoes. She explained how she had triple checked all the numbers and cross checked them against all the relevant government databases.

Jason looked at the numbers, this time patiently, with the eye of an investigator. With each page he turned over, his eyes widened. "Jesus," he murmured under his breath as he continued to stare at the papers. "I don't know how I missed this. How sure are you of these numbers?"

"One hundred percent," she replied with confidence.

Jason leaned back and closed his eyes. The twisted look on his face showed his concern. After what appeared to Marianne to be a long time, he started to slowly nod his head, "You're right. This isn't normal. Something's going on at St. Luke's."

Chapter 2

In his office, located on the tenth floor of St. Luke's Memorial Hospital, a tanned Dr. Mark Coleus, stood by his window and slowly sipped on his first coffee of the day. Having recently just returned from a '*Business*' trip to the Bahamas, his warm, brown coloring, had already started to fade. From his perch, he took his time as he looked out over the work site down below. He enjoyed picturing just what the newest addition to the hospital would look like.

As the recently appointed head of the Cardiology Department, he had worked tirelessly to get the 'Hospital Board of Directors' to approve the new wing devoted to cardiac care. In return, the board, as a sign of their gratitude for all his hard work, had unanimously decided to name the new addition, *'The Mark Coleus Wing'*. It was his intention that it would be the finest center for the treatment of heart disease in the country. With the architectural drawings scattered around his office, Dr. Coleus had studied them so often that he knew each and every one of the fifteen floors by memory.

When he had first proposed the expansion to the Board, he was met with a fair bit of resistance. They hesitated, worried that a new addition wasn't going to be cheap to build. It took a lot of frustrating work to convince the board that the need for a Heart Care Center was there and that the revenue that it would generate would be astronomical.

The gold-colored shovel he had used during the ground breaking ceremony for the new addition hung on his wall. Slightly above the shovel hung a picture taken of the event. He remembered it fondly. They had all come, eager to have their picture taken with him. Pictured with shovels in hand, were his new friend, Mayor Shultz and his wife Grace, along with a couple of State Senators and the main dignitary, Governor Peter Maxwell. They all flashed huge smiles for the cameras. Mark counted himself as being lucky, he was on a first name basis with Mayor Shultz, and his wife. He remembered how the Mayor had sung his praises during the ceremonial speeches. It had been a wonderful day; one he was sure he'd never forget.

The smile he had on his face quickly turned to a frown when he glanced across his office towards his desk. It was piled high with paperwork that had accumulated while he was away on his so called '*Business*' trip. The trip had been a gift. Now that his dream expansion had become a certainty, he found he was being flooded with special favors. When the offerings were being thrown his way, he had known he should have returned them. He knew they were from groups vying for a chance to have a piece of the lucrative hospital expansion contracts. His wife, Alex, had convinced him that he deserved the gifts. After all, that was how big business was done. He agreed with Alex when she told him it was far better if he was the one who received the special attention rather than some faceless hospital administrator who had done nothing towards making the expansion a reality.

Doctor Coleus sat behind his desk and started to go through the piles. Paper, paper, paper, nothing but bloody paper he thought to himself as he thumbed through the stack. From what he could see, there didn't appear to be anything important, just all the usual stuff. There were a number of daily reports of the usage of supplies. Some requisitions for inventory replacements that needed his signature were there. Every time he had to do paperwork; he would get annoyed. He didn't see why he had to waste his valuable time doing such mundane tasks that any office clerk could easily do. There was one piece of paper that he did want, however. The hospital weekly 'Mortality Report' was missing.

The report was not supposed to be released until he had signed off on it. For the last couple of weeks, he had noticed an alarming upward trend in sudden unexplained patient deaths. With his new friend, Mayor Shultz, taking such a special interest in his expansion project, he had taken to quietly adjusting the death numbers. He wanted no negative reports circulating that might jeopardize the city money that Shultz was throwing his way,

He would have asked his assistant about the report, but he had fired her just before he had left on his trip. He had found out the little gossip had been spreading rumors among the nursing staff about private goings on in his Cardiology Department. Rumours, although true, he felt were extremely unfair and downright cruel. All he could think must have happened was that while he was away, enjoying the sun, some fill in office temp must have processed the report and sent it on its' way. Now he had to hope that Mayor Shultz wouldn't notice the report and start asking questions.

*****

23 Years Ago

Mary Brompton sat in the visitors room and anxiously waited for word about her husband. It seemed to be taking an awfully long time. The doctor had assured her that everything was going to be alright. It was a simple, routine operation that would take three hours at the most, he had said. As soon as it was completed, he would personally come and tell her the results. Mary looked to the clock on the wall that slowly ticked away the minutes. It was now approaching four hours, and there was no word yet. Silently, to herself, she had begun to pray.

Her son, Andrew, played in the corner of the room, with some old wooden toy blocks that had been left there ages ago. He could see that his mother was upset. She always became very quiet when she was worried. She had told him this morning that they were going to the hospital to see his father, but that hadn't happened. So far all they have been doing is sit in this room. A white coated doctor had come in and talked with his mother, but he never heard what they were talking about. He was growing tired of playing with these silly blocks. A glance at his mother showed him that she was sitting quietly, with her eyes closed, softly mumbling to herself.

*****

The antiseptic smell in the operating room was sharp. It stung their eyes and burned the back of their throats, even through the medical masks they were all wearing.

“Blood pressure normal, heartbeat weak but holding steady,” the anesthetist, Dr. Turner, called out. He was keeping a close eye on the patient, monitoring the all-important vital signs for any change that might be cause for alarm. From his years of experience, he knew, in critical, ‘Life or Death’ heart surgery, things could go very wrong, very quickly.

Stress was nothing new to Dr. Roger Turner. He was used to it. He had trust in the team assembled in the operating room today. They were an experienced group of professionals whom he had worked with many times in the past. The one big unknown was today’s surgeon. Dr. Mark Coleus was a new transfer to the hospital, having supposedly practiced upstate for a short period of time. Turner had an uneasiness about him. He had already expressed his concern to the head of the Cardiology Care Department earlier, before today’s surgery.

*****

“Do you really think it wise to allow Coleus to perform ‘Open Heart Surgery’ when no one in this hospital really knows anything about him?”

Dr. Jonathon Ecker was the gruff, elderly head of the department. He had served his time, paid his dues over the years. Now his job consisted of mostly paper-work and staffing issues. He was a long time removed from the front lines of the operating room. He had recruited Mark Coleus, sight unseen, wanting to snatch him up before any other hospital had a chance. "I don't see any problem," he dismissed Turner's concern. "I've checked his credentials and on paper he appears to be more than qualified."

"On paper!" Roger exclaimed. "My God. You know yourself, there's a world of difference being in the operating room, holding a live, beating heart in your hands, than anything that could possibly be written on a piece of paper."

Dr. Ecker was starting to get annoyed. As head of the Cardiology Department, he wasn't used to having his decisions questioned. "Now calm down," he stated. "I think you're getting a little carried away. I've looked over the patient's chart and to me, it looks to be a very straight forward bypass operation. Granted, at 36, the man's fairly young for 'Open Heart Surgery', but his age should work in his favor. His health record shows no sign of any other medical issue in his past. From what I can see in his file, he's a happily married man with a six-year-old son." Ecker shook his head, "No, I don't see any reason for Mr. Brompton not to come through this with flying colors and go on to live a full and happy life with his wife and son."

Turner wasn't about to let the issue drop. "I don't care what the man's chart says. Healthy or not, once his chest is cracked open and his heart is exposed, we both know, the only thing between life and death is the skill of the surgeon. And right now, as far as I'm concerned, with your Dr. Coleus, that's an unknown."

"Well, this isn't your concern," Dr. Ecker shot back. "The decision is my responsibility and I've made it."

"I hope to God you're right," Roger declared. "If something goes wrong, it might have been your decision, but it'll be a lifetime of pain, especially for the patient's little six-year-old son."

*****

In the scrub room, prepping for the scheduled surgery, Dr. Roger Turner motioned for the nurse, Lucy Spencer, to come closer to him. He wanted to talk to her quietly, without being overheard.

"Lucy," he whispered, as he scrubbed his hands, working them hard, till they were covered with a white foamy lather. "I have a bad feeling about today."

Nurse Spencer took a step back in surprise. "What do you mean, *'a bad feeling'*?" She had worked in the operating room with Dr. Turner on many occasions and this is the first time he had ever mentioned anything about having a *'bad feeling'*.

"I want you to keep a close eye on Dr. Coleus in there. You've handled more 'Open Heart Surgeries' than just about anyone. If you see anything, and I do mean anything, that doesn't look right, let me know right away."

The concern the doctor was showing put a touch of worry in the mind of the professional nurse. Did Turner know something she didn't? She had never worked with this new doctor, Doctor Coleus, before, but he seemed alright. In the preoperative briefing, he had known all the right words to say as he correctly laid out his plan for the surgery they were about to do. She never picked up on anything that would have been out of order. But now, the comments raised by Doctor Turner, had heightened her awareness.

When Dr. Coleus finally entered the scrub room to begin his preparations, Lucy noticed he appeared to be quite bright and cheerful. His mood gave no indication that he had any worry or concern about the task that lay before of him.

"Morning nurse," he greeted Lucy.

Lucy wasn't sure if his '*nurse*' greeting was because he didn't know her name or if it was because he wanted to keep their working relationship on a formal basis.

"Morning, Dr. Coleus," she replied.

"Is everything ready and in place?"

"Yes doctor," Lucy answered.

"Good. This should be quick. It's a pretty common bypass. I'm not expecting any problems. With a little luck, we should be done this in record time. I tend to work fairly quickly," he bragged. "I have a golf game scheduled for this afternoon that I don't want to be late for," he added. "I hope you and your team can keep up with me," he grinned at the nurse, as Lucy began to pull her medical mask on.

Dr. Turner heard the conversation between Coleus and Lucy. The light heartedness and apparent lack of concern Coleus was showing, did nothing to ease his feelings of uneasiness.

Coleus noticed that Dr. Turner seemed to be staring at him. "Dr. Turner, isn't it?" he asked.

Roger nodded but never said a word.

"Well, come on doctor. Let's get a move on. Get in there and put the patient under. I don't want to be wasting time standing here looking at each other," he ordered.

With the order that Coleus had thrown his way, Roger realized he had more than a '*bad feeling*', he also had just developed a case of '*lack of respect*' for his fellow doctor.

*****

Before administering the anesthetic to the man laying on the operating table, Dr. Turner checked the name tag fastened around the man's wrist, "Darel Brompton" he announced. Nurse Spencer also checked the name tag to confirm the man's name "Darel Brompton," she repeated. With everything checked and in order, Dr. Turner, slowly eased the man into a long, deep sleep.

Through the operating room door, Dr. Coleus, paraded in as if he was some kind of matador entering an arena. Taking his place beside the operating table, he started to bark out orders. “Nurse, adjust the light, I’m operating on his chest not his abdomen,” he said sternly. “And put the drape on him. For God’s sake, do I have to tell you everything?”

Nurse Lucy was stunned. As she placed the green sterile drape across the man’s chest, she couldn’t believe the light hearted doctor she had met in the scrub room had gone through such a Jekel to Hyde conversion in just a mere matter of minutes.

With the patient’s pale white chest now clearly exposed, Dr. Coleus, held his hand out.

“Scalpel,” he snapped.

With one quick slash of the razor-sharp knife, Coleus, peeled back the skin to reveal the sternum lying beneath it.

“Come on nurse, you need to pick up the pace,” he said annoyed. “Cracker.”

Nurse Lucy snapped the tool into the doctor’s hand.

The sound of a loud crack followed quickly by a couple of crunches, filled the room as the rib cage was opened up. “There it is,” he declared as he looked into the open cavity to see the heart beating away.

The operation continued under the watchful eyes of Nurse Spencer and Dr. Turner. Everything was proceeding like a finely oiled machine. Just as Lucy’s worry and Roger’s fears began to lessen, Dr. Coleus glanced up at the clock. “This is taking way too long. We’re already at the four-hour mark and we should have been closing him up at three,” he exclaimed in frustration. The doctor was losing his concentration, trying to rush, as he kept glancing at the moving clock instead of paying attention to what he was doing.

“Wait. Stop!” Nurse Spencer called out to the doctor. “You’re cutting the wrong artery.”

“What?” Dr. Coleus replied, startled by the nurse’s warning. The scalpel cut and blood spurted.

“Blood pressure dropping,” Dr. Turner called out in alarm.

A steady stream of warm blood shot up out of the heart cavity, coating Coleus’ gown and sticking to his face mask. “Now look what you’ve done,” the doctor yelled at Lucy. “I can’t see what I’m doing.”

“Do something now!” Dr Turner screamed. “You’re losing him.”

“For God’s sake, hurry up and wipe my face mask, I can’t see a thing,” Coleus ordered to Lucy.

Dr. Turner stepped away from his position, shaking his head in disgust as he watched Lucy struggle to clean Dr. Coleus' mask. "There's no point, he's gone."

"Damn it nurse, I'll see you pay for your shoddy work," Dr. Coleus threatened Lucy.

"Me!" she replied in surprise. "Clearly you weren't paying attention to what you were doing. I tried to warn you that you were about to cut the wrong artery."

"Don't try to cover up your failings," Coleus stated. "You panicked and caused this to happen with your yelling."

Lucy looked to Dr. Turner in amazement, unable to believe Dr. Coleus was attempting to blame her for the unnecessary death of the patient.

*****

In Doctor Ecker's office, Turner was furious. "I warned you. I told you it was a mistake to have an unknown doctor perform such 'Life and Death' surgery before he proved himself. But you wouldn't listen. You thought you knew better and you said that you would take the responsibility for your decision. Well, your decision has resulted in the needless death of a patient. A wife now has no husband, and worse of all, a six-year-old little boy has no father."

Jonathon Ecker waited until Turner had completed his ranting. He knew there was no point in trying to stop the rage. It was far better to let Turner get everything off his chest. “Dr. Turner,” Ecker started. “I know you’re upset, but this isn’t the way for a professional to act. I’ve read the summery report filed by Dr. Coleus. He indicates the patient’s death was the direct result of the incompetence of the nurse, Lucy Spencer.”

Turner jumped to his feet, “Don’t you even try to blame Nurse Spencer. Don’t forget, I was there. I witnessed firsthand exactly what happened.”

Dr. Ecker didn’t want to get into a contested death situation with the Hospital Board of Review. “As I see it, there are two ways this death can be handled. I can let Dr. Coleus’s summery stand. If I do, that will mean that the Nurse Spencer would be reprimanded and be released from her job. It would also probably result in her losing her Nursing Licence.” He paused to let his words sink into Roger. “Now I’m sure neither of us wants that to happen. I suggest the report be modified to stress that the patient’s heart was in too frail a condition to withstand the operation.”

“You want to sweep this under the carpet?” Dr. Turner asked in disbelief.

“Just between us,” Ecker answered, “Yes. It’s the only way I can see that Nurse Spencer keeps her job and her record remains unblemished,” Ecker stated. What he failed to mention was it also cleared him of any wrong doing for the decision he had made.

*****

Andrew decided that he would take it upon himself to find where his father was. Outside the waiting room, there were halls and halls and halls. He had no idea where his father was, so he started walking, down one hallway then up the next. There were a number of people scurrying about. Nurses, doctors, visitors all going somewhere. A few were pushing carts with wobbly wheels that made Andrew laugh. A few carried trays filled with colored bottles. It amazed Andrew that no one paid any attention to him. He was free to wander around wherever he wanted. In his child's mind he realized he must have become invisible. He had seen the shows on tv where people in hospitals had become invisible. It must have happened to him.

Down one hallway he stumbled upon a group of nurses who were huddled together, talking in whispers amongst themselves. Word had begun to spread quickly among the staff of the death of a heart patient that was being blamed on a nurse. In his believed, childhood invisible state, Andrew giggled as he moved right up beside one of the matronly nurses without even being seen.

' ... *and Dr. Coleus cut the poor man's artery, then tried to blame poor Lucy* ...', ' ... *you should have seen it, there was blood shooting everywhere* ...', ' ... *Dr.*

Turner tried to stand up for Lucy, but I don't think it will do any good ...' '... Oh yeah, old Ecker will stick up for his new golden boy Coleus ...'

Although Andrew could hear what the nurses were saying, he didn't understand what all the fuss was about. A doctor had killed someone and blamed a nurse. He was sure this type of thing happened on tv all the time. Unable to locate where the Doctors had hidden his father, he decided he had better return to the waiting room and be with his mother. When he got there, the white coated doctor had just finished talking with his mother. She had collapsed in her chair and was openly crying. He ran up to her, but she was crying so hard, her tear-filled eyes couldn't see her son. Andrew knew what the problem had to be; he was still invisible to those around him.

Chapter 3

Present Day

A year ago, when she had first moved into her new one-bedroom apartment, it had proven to be a pleasant surprise to Claire. It was so unlike the last place where she had lived. This apartment was bright and airy with rooms large enough for her to walk around without the feeling of being caged in. And the feature she liked the most about her new apartment, was that the closets were huge. There was plenty of room for all the shopping she loved doing. The rent was reasonable and would be easily covered by the wages of her new job as Sergeant of Homicide at the Department of Police Services. With some careful budgeting, at the end of each month she would have just enough money left over to treat herself.

*****

The Department of Police Services office building was a sleek newly designed complex. It's towering walls of glass, set in glimmering panels of black marble, stood out from the other aged buildings that surrounded it. Today, clouds had crept in, giving the building an ominous look and spoiled Claire's view of the river below her office window. She didn't notice the view however, because a note that the department had recently received, disturbed her. When she checked the envelope, she could see that it was addressed to the Police Commissioner, Harold Baywright and he had forwarded it on to her.

Picking up her phone, she dialed. "Is he in? I need to see him right away."

The receptionist recognized the urgency in Claire's voice. "He's free at the moment, but you'll have to come right now. He has an appointment with the County District Attorney soon."

"I'll be right there," Claire stated.

Claire grabbed the note and rushed out her office door. She travelled straight down the hallway, turned at the end, went through the glass doors and entered the Executive wing of offices. At the frosted glass door with the simple engraved name tag, 'Commissioner – Harold Baywright' she stopped, took a deep breath to calm herself, then went inside.

The receptionist, Nancy, looked up, "That didn't take long. Why I've barely hung up my phone."

“This is important,” Claire blurted out as she waved the note in Nancy’s direction.

Of course, Nancy recognized the note. At her boss’s direction, she was the one that had forwarded it on to Claire.

“Well, take a minute and straighten yourself up,” Nancy advised, one girl to another. “You don’t want to go in looking like you’ve just been through a hurricane, do you?”

Claire took a look at herself. Her blouse had come untucked, her skirt had twisted and her hair was swept across her face. “No, I guess not,” she said as she pulled herself together. “Thanks.”

Nancy gave her a once over glance, “That’s better,” she said with a smile. “Go on in.”

Claire approached the inner door and gave a single knock.

“Come.”

She entered to be greeted by the Commissioner.

Harold Baywright was an older man, slightly balding on the top. She guessed him to be in his late 50’s, maybe early 60’s, and today he was wearing a brown tweed jacket, white shirt with a matching brown bow tie. Being a small man, the enormous desk he was sitting behind, gave the impression that there was room for two to three people to be able to use it comfortably. "Sergeant Reindle, what can I do for you?"

"Commissioner Baywright," Claire began. "This note you forwarded on to me was on my desk this morning. I'm confused, why did you send it to me?"

The Commissioner sat back in his chair and struck a fatherly pose. "You work in homicide, don't you?"

"Yes," she replied, a little annoyed with the question. "This obviously is a crank note. We get dozens of these kinds of notes every week. If we followed up on every one of these, we'd never get any real work done."

Baywright stared at his Sergeant. "I don't think this is the work of a crack pot. Did you read the note? Crack pots don't normally sign and give a return address."

"Well, if you believe what this woman says about her husband's death, why wouldn't the hospital be doing something about it."

"That's another issue that needs to be looked at," Baywright answered. "Besides, there's something about the note that sounds genuine to me. This woman, Mya Bittman, claims her husband went into the hospital for a routine heart procedure. When she saw him in the recovery room, she states he was fine, the operation was a success. But later that night she had a call from the hospital that her husband had died for what she claims to be for no reason."

"What is it you want me to do?" Claire asked.

With a stern look and a clear voice, "I want you to do your job, investigate! If there is any truth to what this woman is saying, then I want to know about it."

*****

Back in her office, Claire re-read the note. "Mona," she called out to the department clerk. She didn't wait for a reply, "See if you can get hold of Morrison and Swan. Tell them I want to see them."

"On it," Mona called back.

Claire knew this was going to be a complete waste of time. Her one satisfaction, she thought, chuckling to herself, was that she'll get to tell the Commissioner … *'I told you so.'*

*****

"You wanted to see us Sarge?" Detective Swan asked as he and his partner filled her doorway, blocking the light from entering.

"Come in, close the door and sit down," Claire said.

The two men didn't walk over to the chairs, they lumbered. They were so big that Claire often grimaced to herself, '*I pity what your mothers must have gone through*'.

When the two detectives finally settled into the leather chairs, “We received a note from a wife who thinks the hospital killed her husband,” Claire stated.

Swan and Morrison looked at each other. “You can’t be serious?” asked Morrison. Then sarcastically added, “Of course hospitals kill people, that’s what they’re there for.”

Swan started to give a belly laugh when his Sergeant cut him off. “Alright, I know what you’re thinking, but the Commissioner has ordered us to follow up,” Claire explained.

“Come on, what are we supposed to do with it?”

Claire had been thinking before the two had arrived at her office. While she needed to be thorough enough to satisfy the Commissioner, she also didn’t want to waste a lot of time on the foolish note. “I want you to go interview this Mya Bittman and hear her story firsthand. Then I want you to find out which nurses were on duty at the hospital that night and talk to them.”

Chapter 4

Nurse Michele Rice, sat at her nursing station, sipping on her cup of coffee. She hated having to work the graveyard shift, and this was the third one in a row. Around her, the bells and buzzers were chiming. But they were always chiming. Patients wanted their pillows fluffed, or they wanted their bed raised or lowered and they always wanted to use the bed pan. Well, tonight, Michele was tired and decided the patients would all have to wait. Her feet were sore and her back ached. She needed a few minutes to herself to finish her coffee just once before it got cold.

When she was married, she was Michele Hoover, but that didn't work out. Before she married her husband, he had promised that he would take care of her. He promised her that they would own a nice house in the suburbs and live a good life. She had bought into his promises hook line and sinker. But, once married, it had all turned out to be a lie. Her husband, Mario, had proven to be a dreamer. He always had the perfect scheme that was going to make him millions. All he had managed to really do was to drain her of her life's savings, and then when she had no more money left to give, he up and left her. Stranded alone, with no money, she had only a string of debts left by Mario to remind her of her married life.

Now at thirty-two, Michele was an easy-going woman, in the prime of her life. She was slim, attractive with an amazing pair of long legs that she was very proud of. When she dressed to impress, it was her legs she made sure she showed. This was the time in her life when she had thought she would be traveling the world, having backyard BBQs with interesting friends or be lounging somewhere by a pool in the warm sun. Instead, she had been forced to go back to work and handle damn bed pans. It wasn't fair! She didn't just hate having to work night shifts, she hated her life.

"Excuse me."

Michele looked up to find the night orderly had suddenly appeared out of nowhere and was now standing directly in front of her.

"I'm sorry," he said. "I hope I didn't scare you."

He hadn't scared her. His intrusion annoyed her. Here was someone else to bother her with some crisis that would cause her coffee to turn cold, again.

"I thought you should know that Mr. Haughton, in Room 407, appears to be in a lot of pain. Is there anything you can do for him?"

Michele took a moment and had a good look at the orderly. He appeared to be quite handsome, in a childish way, she thought. His hair was a pile of dark tangled curls resting on the top of his head. His chubby cheeks had the pink flush of a baby. His body wasn't at all muscular. It looked to her like it was soft and would be nice to cuddle with. Putting her coffee down, she was curious.

"Who are you and why are you concerned about Mr. Haughton?"

"I'm Andrew, Andrew Brompton. I'm the night orderly for this floor," he answered. "I just happened to be passing by room 407 and I heard the man moaning. I asked him if there was anything I could do but he never answered, only continued to moan, so I was hoping you could help him."

Michele listened and heard a tenderness in Andrew's voice that she hadn't heard in a long time. Normally she wouldn't even think of telling a stranger about any of her patients, but the care that she felt radiate from Andrew deserved an answer.

She took a quick look around to make sure no one was within ear shot, "I'm sorry to say there's not too much I can do to help Mr. Haughton. He's approaching the end of his life and there is very little hope for him."

Michele thought she could see tears start to well up in Andrew's eyes.

"That's so sad," he said. "I hate to see people suffer all alone. Do you think it would be alright if I sat with him for awhile?"

"Don't you have some work you should be doing?" Michele asked.

"It's alright, I'm on my break," he answered.

For some reason, Michele didn't know why, she felt she didn't want to disappoint this man. "Alright, but only for a little while." Then she added, "And don't touch anything."

Andrew nodded in agreement. Then, just as silently as he had appeared, he disappeared down the hall.

*****

At the end of her shift, Nurse Rice completed her End of Shift Report.

"How was it last night?" Berna, the day nurse asked her as her shift was about to begin.

"All in all, it was a quiet night I guess," Michele answered. "The usual stuff. I think you'll need to keep an eye on Mr. Jenkins in 410. I caught him up wandering around again."

"It's too bad they don't allow us to use restraints anymore," her relief joked.

Then, as she was leaving, "Oh, I almost forgot. Mr. Haughton in 407 finally passed away," she added with an almost flippant tone to her voice. "The night orderly just wheeled him out for the morgue a little while ago." She didn't think it was important to mention that the night orderly, Andrew, had spent time alone, in room 407, with Mr. Haughton.

*****

Michele, restless, tossed and turned in her bed. After working a night shift, she always found it difficult to fall asleep. It just wasn't natural for her to have to work all night, then to be forced to sleep all day.

Her apartment, on the second floor of a rundown, brick three-floor walk-up, wasn't located in the best part of the city, but it was all she could afford. Being firmly in the city's core, it had a number of drawbacks. City traffic was busy and constant. The noise from all the cars at times was overbearing. Sounds of screeching tires with blaring horns never stopped, even long into the night. The sidewalks in the area had become home to an ever-increasing number of vagrants. Wineos and drug addicts could often be found camped out on the stairs leading into her building. Behind them they left the biting odour of urine to flood the building doorway. She dreaded each day and especially each night when she had to run the gauntlet to get to the corner bus stop.

The inside of her apartment was small and cramped. The unmistakable smell of her cats permeated the stale air inside. Cat hair covered the only piece of furniture in her living room. There was no air conditioning. In a futile attempt to keep out the street noise, she had to keep the few windows she had, closed tight, which caused the heat of the day to turn the inside of her apartment into a sweat box. In the middle of the summer, there was nowhere for her to escape the sweltering heat.

It hadn't always been like this. In the early days of her marriage to Mario, they had a wonderful home. Two floors, two baths with space waiting to be filled with little children. But the children never happened, and the house had to be sold to cover the debts left by her husband. There was no question she was lonely. If there had been children, at least there would have been some joyful noise instead of the unbearable drone of the city, that constantly surrounded her.

Lying in her bed, wearing a tattered pair of old striped pyjamas, she stared at her ceiling. There was a crack in the plaster that ran from one corner of the room, over her bed, then down to the door frame. Over the course of many weeks, she had spent hours watching that crack grow, waiting for it to open up and bury her in her bed, beneath a layer of ancient plaster.

Today, as she watched the crack, hoping for sleep to come, she found herself thinking about the orderly from last night. In some sort of weird way, he had struck a chord with her. In her mind, she could see him. She felt he had to be younger than she was, but not that much younger. His baby face with black matted curls on top, hid his age from showing. And she couldn't get the thought out of her head wondering if it would be warm and comforting to snuggle tightly with his chubby body. Her two cats scratched and pawed at her covers. They demanded she move over to give them room to settle comfortably on her bed. She remembered the orderly had told her his name was Andrew something or other. She mustn't have been paying close attention when he told her his last name because she couldn't remember it. The one thing she did remember, as sleep finally started to take hold of her was, that she would have to find out his last name when she saw him again.

*****

Andrew sprawled out on his oversized couch, in the family room of his mother's house. She had passed away sometime ago, leaving the family home to him. In front of him the tv was showing the early morning children's cartoons. He wasn't really watching them; they were just on to keep him company. On the coffee table beside him, there was the half-eaten bowl of cereal that he had started but never finished. Had his mother still been alive, he knew she would have scolded him for not having a coaster under his cereal bowl. '*It will leave a water mark ring if you don't use a coaster*' she would say. The little tabletop displayed a maze of water rings since she had left.

Andrew was awake. Without his mother to tell him when it was time to go to bed or time to get up, he rarely slept. Now he existed through a series of short naps. Throughout the day or night, he would go until he would collapse from exhaustion. A quick nap and he'd be up, ready to go again.

After his first father died on the hospital operating room table, twenty-three years ago, his mother had married again. During a vacation she had taken with her then, teenaged son, Andrew, to Columbia, she had met and fallen in love with Jaun Lopez. Once they were married, she had changed her name to Lopez, but Andrew never did. He never really got along with his stepfather Jaun. He was jealous of him. For most of his life, it had only been Mary and Andrew, mother and son, and Andrew liked it that way. When this new man married his mother, Andrew was squeezed out. Jaun always came first and Andrew was always second.

Unfortunately for his mother, Jaun never lasted long. He had become gravely ill and was confined to his bed. Mary then focused all of her attention caring for her husband and Andrew, for the most part, was left to fend for himself.

Andrew watched as his stepfather Jaun, suffered a long, slow painful death. Although he wasn't particularly friends with Jaun, it bothered him to see his stepfather beg his mother to help bring an end to the suffering. He felt the pain his stepfather felt. He also felt the overwhelming anguish his mother experienced because she was unable to take the pain away from her husband.

When Jaun finally succumbed to his disease, Andrew became aware of the peace that descended upon his mother. A peace that had lifted a tremendous weight from the one person he loved.

Chapter 5

Hearing her doorbell ring startled Mya. Having just finished her afternoon lunch, she had drifted off in a nap. She wondered who would be at her door. Since her husband had passed away, there was rarely anyone who rang the doorbell. She spent the majority of her days and nights alone, with just the company of her tv set.

When she answered her door, she had fully expected to find some religious group trying to save her, but instead, had to look up to see who was talking to her.

"Mrs. Bittman?" Swan asked.

Hesitantly Mya answered, "Yes."

"My name is Detective Julian Swan and this is my partner Detective Tony Morrison. We are from the Police Homicide Group. Did you recently write a note to the Police Commissioner?"

"I certainly did," Mya stated. "I wrote it last week."

"May we come in? We have a few questions we'd like to ask you concerning your note, if that's alright?"

Mya stepped back and opened the door as far as it would go to allow the two men to enter. "Go on into the kitchen," she directed. "We can sit at the table."

The detectives crossed over into the kitchen. Although it was rather small, it was bright and cheerful which made it seem bigger than it really was. A chrome table along with four chairs was strategically placed in one corner of the room. Detective Morrison noticed there were no smells that you would normally expect to have in a kitchen. In his house, with his wife, constantly having to cook and feed their three growing boys, warm enticing aromas would always be floating in the air. He decided that the Bittman kitchen was a room that was very rarely used.

"Would you gentlemen like a coffee? It will only take me a minute," Mya asked hopefully, glad to have the company.

"No, thank you," Julian answered. "We only have a few questions then we can get out of your hair."

"Are you sure? I have everything right here," Mya said. She was in no hurry to have her guests leave.

"I'm sure. It's very nice of you, but we really just need to follow up on your note."

Mya let out a sigh of disappointment as she joined the detectives at the table.

Tony took out his notepad to write as his partner began. "Mrs. Bittman, according to your note, your husband recently passed away."

The mention of her husband caused Mya's eyes to start to water. "Yes, he passed away two weeks ago."

Detective Morrison stopped his writing for a moment, "We're terribly sorry for your loss."

"Thank you."

"Mrs. Bittman," Julian continued. "In your note you say you have concerns about your husband's passing. If it's not too painful, could you tell us about it?"

It took Mya a minute to realize the detective had been talking to her. She had drifted off in a memory and hadn't heard a thing Julian had said to her.

"Sorry, what did you say?"

Julian repeated the question to the woman, "In your own words, could you tell us about your concerns?"

Tony, with his pencil at the ready, waited for the woman to start talking.

"My husband didn't die,' Mya declared in a firm voice. "He was murdered in that hospital!"

*****

"We'll need to have Mona find the home addresses for the two nurses who were on duty that night," Tony stated. "I don't know about you, but if there's even some small bit of truth in what Mrs. Bittman told us, we'll definitely need to talk with those two nurses."

Seeing her two detectives back at their desks, Sergeant Reindle strode out to talk with them. "Were you able to interview Mrs. Bittman?"

Detective Morrison looked up, "We just came back from interviewing her. I can tell you; I feel kind of sorry for her. According to her, she and her husband had been living a dream life. That was until he went to his doctors' for a routine medical check-up. His doctor apparently detected a minor heart issue and sent him to see a specialist." Tony checked his notes, "A Doctor Mark Coleus at St. Luke's Hospital. He'd recently been appointed as head of the Cardiology Department there."

Claire stood confused, "Sounds to me that everything worked as it was supposed to work. I still don't see what the issue is or why the Commissioner wanted us to be involved in this."

"We still have a lot of items to check up on, but I can tell you, that woman is convinced her husband was murdered," Julian said. "Mrs. Bittman had been assured that the procedure was very minor in nature and her husband would be released from the hospital within 24 hours. But instead, when everything appeared to be going well, her husband suddenly, in the middle of the night, died for no apparent reason."

The Sergeant grimaced, "This is going to take up so much time. Well, we have to see it through. What are your next steps?"

"Like you suggested, we're going to interview the two nurses that were on duty on the ward, the night Mr. Bittman died."

Claire thought for a moment, "I think you should also interview this Doctor Coleus. I'd be interested to find out what he has to say about the sudden death."

*****

Who in the world would be bothering her on her day off, thought Michele. The loud noise coming from her apartment door sounded more like someone pounding on it rather than politely knocking.

"Hold on, hold on, I'm coming," she hollered. Carefully, she opened her door, not wanting either of her cats to escape. Alarmed at the two gorillas standing in her doorway, she immediately took a protective step backwards.

"Are you Ms. Michele Rice and do you work as a nurse at St. Luke's Memorial Hospital?" the one asked.

Michele never answered the question. She just stood frozen and stared at the two men. With a slight tremble in her voice, “Who are you?” she asked.

Detective Swan introduced himself and his partner as they both flashed their badges towards her.

Cautiously she asked, “What is it you want?”

“If you’re Michele Rice, then we need to ask you a few questions concerning St. Luke’s Hospital. If we could come in, I promise you this won’t take very long, then we can be on our way.”

When Michele reluctantly opened her door to allow the men to enter, Detective Swan winced and his eyes began to water from the overwhelming sour smell of cats and their damn litter boxes that assaulted him.

“I’m sorry, I don’t have many chairs, I live alone and have never needed any.”

Swan and Morrison completely filled the worn, stuffed couch, while Michele sat on a small wooden side chair she often used as a side table, that rested at one end of the couch. Detective Swan grimaced as a large silver-gray Persian cat began rubbing up against his pant leg.

“Ms. Rice,” Detective Swan started as his partner began writing in his notebook. “We’d like to ask you a few questions concerning the night shift you worked when a Henry Bittman passed away.”

Michele thought for a moment, "That was well over two weeks ago. Why in the world would you want to know about that now?"

Not wanting to give too much away, "Just a routine matter we need to clean up," Julian replied. "Can you walk us through everything you can remember about that night. We're particularly interested in anything you can remember about Mr. Bittman?"

"I don't know. Two weeks ago, during a night shift is pretty difficult. When you're working night shifts, after awhile they all start to run together, you know."

"Please try. Just do the best you can," Swan urged as he gave the Persian a subtle nudge with his leg in a foolish attempt to push it away.

"Let's see. As far as I can remember, it was a quiet night. Of course, there was the usual bell ringing from patients wanting different things, but nothing out of the ordinary. I was working with Caroline Mauro. I probably shouldn't mention this, but she was more than a little hung over from a family birthday party, if I'm remembering right. So, I let her rest and drink coffee most of the night while I answered the majority of the calls."

"And did Mr. Bittman ring his call bell for anything during the night?" Swan asked.

“No, but being on the Cardio ward, we take each of the patients' vitals every two hours. Mr. Bittman slept soundly and his vitals were normal.”

Detective Morrison stopped writing for a moment and asked, “Other than Nurse Mauro and yourself, do you remember if there was anyone else present on the ward that night?”

“I don’t think so,” Michele tried to remember. “During night shifts you’re pretty much on your own.” Then she added, “Of course there was the normal Housekeeping Staff. They use the night time to do the majority of their cleaning when there’s nobody around to bother them.”

“And by chance do you happen to remember any of their names?” Tony asked hopefully.

“No idea. I’ve only been working at St. Luke’s for a little over a month, so I haven’t had time to get to know any of them. They come and they go. I’m usually too busy to pay any attention to them anyway. I think that if you check with the Housekeeping Office, you may be able to find out who was assigned to our floor that night.”

“We’ll do that,” Swan replied.

“Oh, I almost forgot. Usually our orderly, Andrew Brompton is around. But I can’t say for certain if he was on the floor that night. He’s such a nice caring young man. Sometimes, when he has a break, he'll sit and talk with the patients."

Detective Morrison never said anything but made a point of circling the orderly's name in his notepad.

"Now can you tell us about the time when Mr. Bittman actually passed away?" Detective Swan asked.

"Sure. Like I said, Caroline was resting and I was taking the patient calls. At about two in the morning, the monitor alarm for Mr. Bittman went off. I was at the other end of the ward and I couldn't leave the patient I was with. I assumed that Caroline would answer the alarm. Well, by the time I got to Mr. Bittman's room, couldn't have been more than a couple of minutes, I found Caroline on Mr. Bittman's bed preforming chest compressions. As soon as I entered the room, I could tell Mr. Bittman was gone."

"Did you see anyone else anywhere near the room?" Tony asked.

"No. The only other person that I'm aware of who entered the room was Dr. Fletcher. But that was a good half hour later. He had to come to declare that the patient was dead," Michele remarked.

"Do you remember what was listed as the official cause of death?" Julian asked.

Michele looked surprised at the question as she slowly stroked an orange tabby cat that had jumped up on her lap. To her, the cause of death was pretty obvious. “Heart failure!” she answered.

*****

“Just move those drawings over there,” Dr. Coleus directed to the two detectives as they looked around his office trying to find somewhere to sit. “I can only spare you a couple of minutes,” he said as he glanced down at his watch. “I was away this past week and I have a lot of work to catch up on.”

“We won’t take much of your time,” Detective Swan assured him. “We only need to ask a few questions.”

The sooner he was able to get rid of these two, the better, Coleus thought to himself. He had planned to pay a visit with the Mayor and didn’t want to be late. He had decided that his best course of action was to talk face to face with his friend concerning the alarming number of sudden deaths the hospital had been experiencing lately. He wanted the Mayor to hear it from him personally rather than read about it on the front page of the local papers.

“Dr. Coleus, it is our understanding that recently, you personally looked after a Henry Bittman as a patient here at the hospital. Is that right?” Detective Morrison asked.

Coleus was wary of the question and hesitated in his answer. "Why would police detectives be asking questions about any of my patients?" he asked the two.

"Nothing to worry about," Detective Swan tried to reassure the doctor. "We just have a few loose ends from a routine matter we are hoping you could help us with."

Coleus thought for a moment. He didn't rise to become the head of the largest Cardiac Care Facility in the county in such a short period of time by being a fool. If these two were asking questions about his patient, they were after something and he needed to figure out what it was before he answered anything. Thoughts started whirling round in his brain. Was it because of the rumours his ex-assistant had started? Was it because one of his staff had complained about him? Or was it because some relative of one of his patients was preparing to launch a 'Malpractice' lawsuit against him? He knew any of these could be devastating to his expansion project. While he felt he might be able to explain one thing to the Mayor, if scandals started piling up, one on top of another, that would be a different matter. A matter that might very well turn the glorious 'Mark Coleus Cardiac Wing' to dust right here in front of his eyes.

"Gentlemen," Coleus decided it would be better to play it safe, "I don't think I'm at liberty to divulge the medical records of any of my patients. 'Doctor –

Patient' confidentiality is very important in the practice of medicine. Why, if a patient can't trust his doctor, then who can he trust?"

"But Mr. Bittman is dead," Swan stated.

"Never the less, he and his family have a right to privacy."

*****

Sergeant Reindle sat behind her desk and listened to her two detectives. Their report concerning the Bittman letter troubled her.

"I'm telling you, Sarge, I can't put my finger on it but I'm getting a weird vibe on this letter," Detective Swan stated. "I mean, something's just not right."

"Yeah," his partner added. "We've interviewed everyone involved, just like you asked us to do, and my gut is telling me, this doesn't add up."

Claire started drumming her fingers on her desk. This letter was turning out to be a pain, she thought to herself. "I don't understand," she said. With a look towards Swan, "You say something's not right." Then she turned towards Morrison "And you say your gut is telling you it doesn't add up."

'Tap, tap, tap, tap', her fingers drummed on her desk, over and over, as she stared out into space, locked in

deep thought. Slowly her head began to nod back and forth. '*Tap, tap, tap, tap*'.

"I just don't see it," she said. "Think about it. A man has a heart problem. He goes into the hospital. The leading Cardiac doctor operates. During the night, the alarms sound and the nurses try to revive him. The man dies. What more is there?" she asked.

"For a starter," Detective Morrison stated as he looked through his notebook. "Why was Dr. Coleus so vague in his answers? I just don't buy this 'Patient-Doctor' confidentiality bit over a dead man. He's hiding something. Then there's the wife. She insists she was told the operation was very minor and when she saw her husband after the surgery, she claims he was perfectly fine."

"And the nurses," Detective Swan jumped in. "One of them was hung over while the other one does all the work? Yet, it was the hung over one who was doing the CPR because the other one was supposedly busy at the far end of the hall."

"Then there's the cleaners who are wandering around and nobody's paying any kind of attention to them," Tony continued. "And the night orderly, this Andrew Brompton, what kind of orderly spends his breaks, sitting and talking to patients in the middle of the night? Nurse Rice indicated that Bittman was sleeping soundly when she checked on him every two hours. Yet she says this orderly had been in the room talking to the patient." Detective Morrison's voice started to rise, "I tell you; I'm convinced something's wrong here, terribly wrong."

Sergeant Reindle would have liked to end this wild goose chase here, but with both of her detectives so adamant that something was wrong, she was left with no choice. The goose chase would have to continue.

"Alright," she said reluctantly. "Since you two are so convinced that something is wrong with Bittman, here's what we're going to do. First, I'm going to contact the County Medical Examiner. I'll get her to look into the cause of the death. She'll be able to force Coleus to release his medical records. While I'm doing this, I want you two to take a hard look at the doctor. Check everything about him. Check his background. See if there's any skeletons in his closet. Also, quietly check with the people that work with him. Find out what he does during his day, and what do they think about him. I want to put this whole thing to bed once and for all. If he's involved in anything, we need to know now."

Her two detectives listened and nodded their heads in approval. Detective Morrison jotted the Sergeant's orders down as fast as she was firing them off.

"And one other thing," she added. "Just to be sure we have the full picture of this doctor, have a look at all his bank records."

Chapter 6

The small room located in the back section of the Mayor's Mansion, felt like an old boy's club. Several thick high back leather chairs crowded around a cold fireplace. Mark could smell the stink from years of cigar smoke trapped in the stuffy room. Grace, the mayor's wife, sat impatiently in one chair, with a half full whiskey glass balanced on her chair's arm. Her tight face caused the knob of her chin to protrude out. If you met her on a dark night, you'd swear she was about to cackle.

"What's so important you needed to see me right away?" she asked, annoyed at the disruption to her day by this pompous ass of a doctor. Her husband, the Mayor, may have taken a liking to him, but she surely hadn't.

"I was hoping to talk privately with the Mayor," Coleus said meekly. He was intimidated by the forcefulness of Grace Shultz.

For Grace, it was hard enough having to work in the background behind her husband. So many people were hangers-on, trying to get a piece of the Mayor for their own gain. If they only knew, Ruger Shultz was a man who was mayor in name only. It took careful planning and a lot of work, on Grace's part, to keep the fact that her husband, was an incompetent oaf from the public. Sure, he looked the part, tall, handsome, and projected an image of steady confidence. But it was all an illusion. He was nothing more than a hollow shell of a man. To those in the know, they knew it was her who really ran the city.

Coleus took a deep breath and started his tale. He danced around in his explanation of the number of recent sudden deaths that were happening at his hospital. He knew the real reason what the cause was, but he didn't want to tell Grace. He was trying to be very careful in what he was saying.

"Stop beating around the bush," Grace demanded sharply. "You came here on some urgent matter you just had to tell my husband personally, now what is it?"

The tone of her voice, the look on her face and the power in her eyes as she tore into him unnerved him. He had no choice but to tell her the truth.

"There's a 'Death Angel' active in the hospital."

"What the hell do you mean, 'Death Angel'?" Grace was quickly losing her temper with this fool. "Talk English for God's sake."

Coleus tried to explain. "In hospitals, the term 'Death Angel' refers to a misguided individual who takes it upon his or herself to prematurely end patients lives, for reasons that are only known to themselves."

Grace wanted more information, "And how many deaths are we talking about?"

Mark, fearfully, in a low shameful voice answered, "Too many!"

"Damn it! We've put a lot of money into that hospital of yours for your bloody expansion. The Mayor has been milking the hospital for all the good press we can get. Why it's caused his rating in the polls to jump several points. And now you're telling me it's all about to blow up in his face?"

Grace, stunned, sunk down deep in her chair. This was the first she had ever heard of an active 'Death Angel'. She knew if this horrific story were to leak out to the press and be used against her husband, it would be crippling. Any bad press or scandal now, when her husband was just coming up for re-election would put her whole lifestyle, her whole image of who she was, in jeopardy. She was the wife of the Mayor, first lady of the city. If this damn story ever got out, she'd be reduced to being the shameful wife of a despicable fool, she thought to herself. The fancy dresses would be gone. The colorful city balls would be gone. The powerful friends, who hung on her every word, would be gone. Something had to be done, and it had to be done quickly.

"What the hell are we going to do?" she asked.

"I've been trying to hide the numbers, but some leaked out in a report last week while I was away," Mark stated. "I could keep changing the number of deaths that get reported." He never mentioned his recent interview with two homicide detectives. He felt that was too much for this woman to handle right now.

"Get serious," Grace replied. "It's already out there. I can see the press headlines now '*Mayor Shultz supports Hospital of Death!*'" Grace took a large swig of fortifying liquor from her glass. "The press would eat the Mayor alive. And remember what Watergate did to Nixon when he tried to cover things up, for God's sake. There has to be another way." Absent mindedly she swirled the remaining colored liquid in her glass, round and round, as she thought. "We'll have to do this without the Mayor being involved," she declared.

"But how?" Mark asked.

"That's not my problem, it's yours," Grace answered. "You're going to have to find and eliminate this so called 'Death Angel' and wipe the hospital records clean."

"It sounds so easy to do when you say it, but that would be putting me in an awful precarious position," Coleus warned.

All the Mayor's wife did was smile and ask, "You do like having your job, don't you?"

Chapter 7

The florescent lights on the ward were blazing. Whether it was day or night outside, you couldn't tell. On the ward, the lights were always on. Nurse Rice, just back at the nursing station from changing the wound bandage on Mrs. Mory in room 412, was taking her time entering the dressing change in the hospital computer system. Since she had started working at St. Luke's Hospital, well over a month ago now, she had received enough lectures. '*Everything must be documented in the system. Every band aid, every Q-Tip, every pill*'. Michele had taken the time necessary to learn how to use the hospital's computer system, knowing full well that it could be an advantage to her. She had been told all the record keeping was necessary so that the hospital could accurately bill the patient's insurance company. It had been drummed into every employee that it was the insurance companies that paid their wages. Every two weeks, when she opened her pay statement, she'd grimace. Somebody must be making a goodly sum but it sure as hell wasn't her. The wages she made barely paid her rent.

She stopped for a moment and drifted back to the day when she was first hired by the Director of Nursing, Doris Hopkins. They had hit it off right from the start. Doris was a 'Cat Lady' just like she was.

On that day, Michele had stepped off the bus, in front of the hospital, at precisely 5 minutes to 10am. She checked the little reminder note she had written to herself. Her appointment was with the Director of Nursing, a Doris Hopkins, located somewhere in the Hospital's Administrative Offices.

She remembered how she had stood in front of the building, as she tried to get her bearings. The building was huge. From where she stood, she couldn't tell how many floors the hospital was. At the time she had guessed there had to be at least twelve maybe fifteen floors.

To her right, the enormous 'Emergency' sign pointed towards the far end of the building. She had noticed how the large sliding doors there were already surrounded by an assortment of ambulances, waiting to be unloaded. In the background she had heard the wailing of sirens that indicated more were on their way. She knew from her experience that it would be another busy day in the 'Emergency Department'. Day or night, it was always busy for the nurses that worked in Emergency.

To her left she had noticed that there was a beehive of activity happening. She remembered taking a moment to watch in awe while a machine, which was nearly twice the size of the bus she had arrived in, had been busily scraping away at the ground. It was filling a steady stream of dump trucks with dirt to be taken away somewhere. Whatever they were gearing up to build, she could tell it was going to be big.

She remembered when she had glanced down at her watch the feeling of panic that had started to fill her. She had realized that she had wasted too much time gawking around and she was now late for her 10am appointment.

When she had stepped inside the hospital front entrance way, she was instantly lost. People were scurrying about, going this way and that. All of them appeared to be in a frantic need to get somewhere. To the side, there was a waiting area filled with people all waiting for something. To Michele it looked like each one of them had their face glued to their phone and were oblivious to the organized chaos that was happening around them. The area in front of her had what at first glance appeared to be something right out of a game show. A maze of corridors jutted off in every direction to confuse her. She had to guess which one to use to reach her desired destination. It had taken a number of tries before she found the right one. She remembered how relieved she had felt as she took a deep breath and finally stepped inside the 'Administrative Offices'.

Today, in her head, that first meeting with Doris played out just as if it was a movie. The memory was so clear and vivid to her that now it made her chuckle. She couldn't believe how needless her worrying had been.

"Can I help you?" the little pixie of a receptionist had asked.

"I'm Michele Rice," Michele replied. "And I believe I have an appointment for 10:00 o'clock about a possible nursing position."

"If you could just have a seat to the side there, Ms. Hopkins will be with you shortly. She's on the phone right now and you can go in as soon as she finishes up on her call. I know she's been expecting you." Then softly she had uttered something that she never should have said, "We're so short of staff now." When the light on her desk phone finally went out, "Looks like she's finished, please go in. I know she's really looking forward to your interview."

As soon as Michele had entered the woman's office, she quickly looked around. She wanted to get a measure of this woman. In front of her, she saw a plain woman, dressed modestly, a little on the frumpy side, with a short, dull brown Bob style of haircut sitting behind an ornate desk. Prominently displayed on the woman's desk, for everyone to see, were two rather large pictures. One, in a portrait style photo, the woman was holding an orange striped cat, that had a monster sized head, both smiling for the camera. Michele could see the cat's face showed more of a look of annoyance than that of any kind of a real smile. The second picture was of another cat. This one, showed a large, overweight black cat, stretched out across an overstuffed, hair covered couch. The display gave every indication that Ms. Hopkins, much like her, was definitely a lonely spinster who had filled her empty life with a love for cats. Michele had decided to use that information to her advantage.

"My what amazing cats you have."

A smile instantly shone across the woman's face. "Oh yes. They're just like my children." Then she asked, hopefully, "Do you like cats?"

The woman had played right into Michele's hands. "Oh, my yes. I have two cats myself. A scraggly little imp I call Mr. Briggs and a silver haired Persian named Ali."

Doris Hopkins smiled as she opened the file which Michele had presented to her.

"Hmm, I see you come quite highly recommended. Very impressive," Doris stated. "Let me see, The Pittsburgh Regional Hospital. I believe the Director of Nursing there is Marla Brooks, isn't it?" she asked. "Marla's an old school mate of mine. I haven't heard from her in a long time," she remarked wistfully.

Michele had decided that she needed to change the subject quickly. She didn't want Doris to notice that she hadn't been nursing for a very long time and that her resume was years old. It was only when that bastard 'Mario' had walked out on her and left her stranded did she have to return to nursing. "My cat, Mr. Briggs, has been out of sorts lately and I'm not sure what to do for him." She wanted to have the woman focus her attention on cats rather than her resume.

"Well," Doris said, happy to offer advice on anything related to the world of cats. "That's because he's a male, isn't it." As Doris looked to the picture of her fat, black cat, Michele noticed the sudden appearance of a scowl that had started to cover the woman's face. "They're just like men, you know. If they're not running around marking their territory, then they're laying around being lazy and getting fat."

From the anger in her voice and the look on her face, Michele knew Doris was no longer talking about cats. She could tell, just like her, this woman had been hurt sometime in her past and the pain still lived strong in her.

Doris had offered her the position of night shift 'Fill in Nurse'. It meant that Michele had to work the night shifts around the whole hospital whenever any 'Regular' nurse was absent. Michele didn't like it, but she had no choice. She needed a job and was willing to take whatever she could get. Doris had promised her it would only be for a little while until a 'Regular' position opened up. "After all," she had said. "We cat people must stick together, don't we!"

The buzzing of the call bells abruptly brought Michele back from her daydream. Mr. Jenkins was up and on the prowl again. '*A few more hours then I'll be out of here'*, she thought to herself.

*****

Andrew absent mindedly picked away at his microwaved dinner that filled a plastic container he held in his lap. It was his usual nightly meal that he had earlier purchased from the corner deli. He missed the tasteful meals his mother used to make for him. She had always prepared her dining room table with china dishes and real cloth napkins. She had been such a good cook. Every meal with her had been a delight. And when he was old enough, she used to share a small amount of rich red wine, served in crystal glasses, with him. They'd each make a toast. His mother's toast would be serious, wishing good health and happiness to her son. His toast was usually silly, wishing they would get a dog or a cat that he could play with and take care of. He remembered how being allowed to share that taste of wine with his mother had made him feel so grown up. But now his mother was gone and he missed her. His microwaved dinners, which he washed down with a bottle of soda as he sat in his chair in front of his tv, were just not the same.

This evening, instead of watching his tv, he found himself thinking about Nurse Rice. While the other nurses would usually ignore him and pretend to not see him, Nurse Rice always made it a point to talk with him. And she was the only nurse that let him sit with the patients. He was lonely. The only people he was ever able to talk with were hospital patients that usually were far too ill to talk with him. The friendliness Nurse Rice showed him, drew him closer and closer to her. He wondered if she was a good cook, just like his mother had been. Then he wondered if Nurse Rice would cook a delicious meal for him. Together they could share some wine and make toasts to each other, all throughout the evening.

Chapter 8

As she drove in her car, Claire kept one hand on the steering wheel while the other busily rooted around in her handbag for her sunglasses. Having to travel to the East side of the city resulted in her having to squint as the bright morning sun shone right through her front window. Compact, lipstick, hair brush, gun, she kept rummaging around. They had to be here somewhere. 'Ahh' she sighed when her fingers finally grasped the elusive pair of glasses. Even though feeling the warmth of a morning sun that harkened a day ahead full of promise would have normally put a smile on her face, she felt today wasn't one of those mornings. It was a damn nuisance, Sergeant Reindle thought to herself as she got out of her car in front of the old Municipal Building. In order to meet with the County Medical Examiner, Dr. Marianne Bevan, she had been forced to travel halfway across the city. Claire knew the doctor had been given the opportunity to relocate into the new Police Services Building when it was being built. But the stubbornness of the doctor, not wanting to move, resulted in everyone else being inconvenienced.

She exited the elevator on the sixth floor, turned left, walked to the end of the hallway and entered the office.

"Sergeant Reindle, so nice to see you," Marjorie, the doctor's assistant, cheerfully greeted her. "You can go right in, she's expecting you."

When Claire entered the inner office, it was as if she had taken a step back in time. The Doctor was there, sitting at her desk in the middle of the room, surrounded by shelves and shelves of books and what looked like to the Sergeant to be the wildest assortment of clutter she had ever seen.

The doctor closed the thick book she had been studying, "Claire, have a seat," she directed to the Sergeant. "Now what's this letter you were telling me about on the phone?"

Claire settled herself in and laid out the complete tale of what was now called 'The Bittman' letter to the Doctor. " ... and the Commissioner has directed my group to investigate. Personally, I think it's a complete waste of time, but he doesn't see it that way."

Doctor Bevan sat back in her chair and tried hard not to smirk at the Sergeant. "You say your two detectives, what were their names, Swan and Morrison, did a preliminary investigation."

"Yes, and although they couldn't find anything definite, they both think there's something wrong with Henry Bittman's death. That's why I've come to see you."

"Oh," Dr. Bevan replied in mock surprise. Until she knew more of what the Sergeant wanted, she had decided to play her cards close to her chest. "What could I possibly do for you? My office hasn't been involved in any aspect of Mr. Bittman's death." Marianne was aware of the man's passing, but until now she didn't know any of the circumstances. She had recognized the name from the Mortality Report issued by St. Luke's Hospital. With the city's homicide group now active in a probe to investigate the sudden death, it added another layer of credibility to her suspicions.

Claire continued, "When my two detectives attempted to interview the Head of Cardiology for the hospital, Dr. Mark Coleus, he stonewalled them. Claimed 'Doctor – Patient' confidentiality, even though Mr. Bittman was dead."

Dr. Bevan took a moment to think. She was well aware of Coleus. The antics of the Doctor had been brought to her attention several times in the past by disgruntled nurses. However, without real proof of 'Malpractice' her hands had been tied. This new information was extremely interesting to her. In her mind, she began to work through the possible scenarios that were now coming to light. *'Was Dr.*

Coleus involved with the 'Death Angel'? If so ... how and why? By claiming 'Confidentiality' was he attempting to hide something? If he was ... then that was something that she was now eager to find out about.'

The Sergeant could see that Dr. Bevan had drifted off into deep thought. "What I'd like to ask you is if you could use the power of your office to force Coleus to release the medical records for Henry Bittman's death? Having those records would be a great help towards my department being able to wrap this whole affair up."

The doctor couldn't contain herself any longer. With a loud chuckle she said, "If I were you, I wouldn't be in such a hurry to close your investigation."

Claire tried to figure out what was so funny to the doctor.

"And," she added, "I'd be thinking about giving your two detectives a raise. They appear to be a lot smarter than you're giving them credit for."

Claire didn't say a word. She just sat there, perplexed by the surprisingly cheerful attitude Doctor Bevan was displaying.

"Give me a minute while I call in my department's investigator," the Doctor said. "You might know him, Jason Adler. We have a few things we really need to tell you about as to what we think may be going on at St. Luke's Hospital.

Sergeant Reindle knew Jason very well. In fact, she knew him so well that she could describe the cherry-colored birthmark on his left inner thigh!

When Jason Adler entered the room, he was surprised to see Claire sitting there with his boss. This was the last place he had expected to find her. When he had last seen her, she had been sitting on the side of the bed with tears streaking down her face. He had just told her that their affair was over. She was too demanding, too possessive and he wasn't ready for any long-term commitment. He remembered it was so hard for him to do, but he had to do it. If he didn't, he felt he would be consumed by her. He could still hear her sobs as he closed the door behind him on that day when he left.

"Jason, I'm not sure if you've met Sergeant Claire Reindle from the Homicide Group," Dr. Bevan said.

With a sullen look on his face, "Yes, the Sergeant and I have met." He turned to look at the Sergeant directly in her eyes, "Hello Claire, what brings you here?"

While Jason might have been a little pensive about seeing Claire, she on the other hand was beaming. Her face flushed with a warmth that quickly spread throughout her body. Seeing this man, being so close to him, brought a flood of memories boiling to the top of her brain. Their affair might have been brief, but to

Claire, it was powerful. Their time together filled every part of the dream life she was looking for. It was a life filled with stolen moments together. There were secret kisses when she thought no one was looking, long walks in the park while holding hands and saying silly words of love to each other. Sometimes their love making had been soft and tender, while other times, it was hot, hard and sweaty, but always it had been wonderful for Claire.

The change that had swept over Claire did not go unnoticed by Dr. Bevan. She could tell there was a far deeper history between these two than just a business relationship. Even though, Jason was years younger than her, Dr. Bevan, surprised herself with the little pangs of jealousy she could feel creep up on her. Casually she got up from behind her desk and moved to position herself between the two.

"Jason, the Sergeant here has been investigating a sudden death that occurred recently over at St. Luke's. Originally, I had thought you could take her to your office and bring her up to speed with our discovery of what we think is going on at St. Luke's." Then, with the firm tone of the one in control, "I now think it might be far better if all three of us were to go to the conference room so we can discuss this fully. Don't you agree Sergeant?"

Claire shot a quick look at the doctor to let her know, *'Old woman, you're playing with fire.'* "If you say so," Claire answered.

"I do, I most certainly do."

Chapter 9

'Code Blue, Fourth Floor. Code Blue, Fourth Floor'.

The hospital loudspeakers blared. In the cafeteria, groups of nurses on their morning coffee break stopped and raised their heads to listen. *'Code Blue, Fourth Floor'.* That's ok, not my floor, each one individually thought, as they ignored the alarm and collectively went back to their chit chatting.

At the sound of the alarm, Dr. Fletcher, with a bagel clamped between his teeth, jumped up from his table and ran for the elevator. A look to the elevator dial showed it was stopped on the tenth floor. He decided he couldn't wait and rushed to the stairwell. Taking two, sometimes three stairs at a time, he charged upward. When he reached the fourth floor, red faced, he stopped and gasped for air. A glance at his hands made him realize he was still holding a half-eaten, crushed bagel in his clenched fist. Down the hallway, he could see the crowd that had gathered outside room 417.

"Excuse me, excuse me! Get out of my way," he called out as he pushed forward to the front of the crowd. Inside the room, the monitor was beeping incessantly as the patient's heartbeat raced at an alarming rate. *'Beep, beep, beep'.* At the bedside, he squeezed himself between two oversized nurses. *'Beep, beep, beep'.*

"Shut that damn noise off," he demanded. "Quickly, what's going on?" he asked as he reached over and lifted the patient's eyelids to check for responsiveness.

Nurse Donna Mackle blurted out, "Fifty-seven years old, recent Cardiac Ablation Operation to stop Atrial Fibrillation. I had just injected the prescribed 'Adrenaline' into his IV, when his heart started to race out of control."

Fletcher leaned over and pressed his stethoscope against the patient's chest. "Adrenaline!" he yelled in disbelief. "Why the hell did you give him Adrenaline for God's sake?"

In her defence she responded, "It was on his chart, ordered by Dr. Coleus."

"He's crashing. Paddles, give me the damn paddles. Come on, come on, quickly," he demanded. With the paddles pressed firmly against the man's still chest, "Clear," he hollered.

"Clear," came the response.

'Thump'

The patient's back arched up from the bed then fell back. No effect. The heart monitor beside the bed continued to draw a straight line across its' green screen.

"Quick," Fletcher demanded towards Nurse Mackle. "Inject 1mg. of Epinephrine."

"Again, once more," he called out, as he worked at a feverish pace. With the paddles still in hand, his movements were a blur as he fought to save the man's life.

"Clear," he screamed, to be heard above the chorus of moans from the doorway crowd.

And again, the response came. "Clear."

'Thump'

The patient's back again arched upwards. Higher than before. Up, up, up towards the ceiling before falling back to the bed.

This time the heart monitor showed a slight shiny '*blip*' which started to grow and move across the screen. The doorway crowd were gripped in silence as they waited to hear ... *'Blip...Blip...Blip'*.

With a deep breath of exhaustion, Dr. Fletcher finally dropped the paddles. "Alright. He's back." A round of applause instantaneously rose from the doorway spectators. A smile of success crept across the Doctor's face, “Okay, okay. Show’s over. Get back to work,” he called out. With a stern look towards Nurse Mackle, “Keep a close eye on him and notify me immediately if there is any change. I’ll be in Dr. Coleus’ office. I can’t believe even he would be stupid enough to order ‘Adrenaline’ for an ‘Afib’ patient.”

*****

“What the hell were you thinking?” Dr. Fletcher demanded as he stormed into Coleus’s office.

Dr. Coleus was startled by the sudden violent intrusion. He was going to have to get a replacement receptionist soon if for nothing else than to stop these annoying interruptions. First there were the two police detectives, trying to pry information out of him about some patient named Bittman, and now this. “You do know it’s customary to knock, don’t you?” he snarled.

“Never mind that,” Dr. Fletcher answered. “You just about killed Mr. Harris.”

“What in the world are you talking about? I performed a standard ablation procedure on the man and he should be able to be discharged today,” Coleus responded. “There were no problems. The operation went like clockwork. When I checked on him this morning, he was resting comfortably.”

Fletcher wasn’t about to give up. Overtime, he had grown increasingly tired of having to fix Coleus’s screwups. “If everything was so fine, then why did you prescribe ‘Adrenaline’ to be administered via IV?”

Dr. Coleus sat for a moment and tried to remember the day’s events. He couldn’t remember anything about ‘Adrenaline’. “What makes you think I ordered the drug? The man suffers from Afib. A dose of ‘Adrenaline’ would more than likely kill him. You don’t want to speed the man’s heart up. You want to slow it down, for God’s sake.”

“Did you not just hear the ‘*Code Blue*’ alarm? That was for your patient, Mr. Harris. He was crashing due to Nurse Mackle having administered a dose of ‘Adrenaline’ to him that she claimed you ordered,” Dr. Fletcher stated. “If I hadn’t shocked him, he’d be dead by now.”

Adrenaline … Adrenaline … Coleus wracked his brain. “There has to have been some mistake. I never ordered any Adrenaline. That Nurse Mackle must have screwed up.”

“Don’t bother trying to shift the blame onto Mackle,” Fletcher stated as he pushed Coleus out of his way. He logged into the computer that was sitting on Coleus’ desk. With a quick search through the patient records system, he found what he was looking for. “See, it’s right here under physician’s orders. ‘0.5ml. of Adrenaline’ to be given by IV. The order has your name on it.”

Dr. Coleus stared at the screen. “That’s not possible. I swear I never entered any such order.”

“Well,” Fletcher stated, with a touch of disbelief in his voice. “If you didn’t do it, then someone has hacked into the system pretending to be you.”

*****

When Sergeant Reindle finally returned to the Police station, she went directly to her office. Her trip to the County Medical Examiner had given her a lot she needed to think about. Alone in her office, with her door closed, she ran through what she had learned.

The simple note that had been passed down to her from the Police Commissioner for the first time weighed heavy on her. Up to now, she could have sworn it was a hoax. She had thought the note was little more than an attempt by a grieving widow who was trying to make some sense out of her husband’s sudden death. Right from the start, everyone around her who had seen the note, felt that it was real. The Commissioner, Baywright, had seen something in the note that she had failed to see. Both of her detectives, Swan and Morrison, still early in their investigation had told her that something wasn’t right, but she didn’t believe them. It wasn’t until the Medical Examiner, Dr. Bevan, had taken the time to explain to her what she believed to be going on over at St. Luke’s Hospital, had she realized the true importance of the Bittman note. Claire’s original thoughts of being able to tell the Commissioner, '*I told you so*', had gone and blown up in her face.

"Swan, Morrison, get in here!" she yelled out in frustration through her closed door.

*****

Once the two detectives had settled into their chairs, Claire took a deep breath. She knew she needed to keep a clear head and not get distracted by her personal failings no matter how much they hurt her.

"I need to apologize to you both," she said. "You were right and I was wrong."

Julian and Tony looked at each other, uncertain as to what the Sergeant was talking about.

Claire continued, "I've just come from a very enlightening meeting with the Medical Examiner, Dr. Bevan."

The two detectives still had no idea what their Sergeant was talking about or what she was leading up to.

"Up to now, I have to confess that I thought this 'Bittman' letter was just an elaborate hoax," she said.

Claire went on to describe her meeting with Dr. Bevan and how the letter was just the tip of the iceberg as to what was believed to be going on at St. Luke's Hospital.

" … Dr. Bevan is sending over the paperwork to order Dr. Coleus to release the medical records of Mr. Bittman. Check with Mona, she might have them already. When you serve the papers to Coleus, I want you to take Bevan's investigator Jason Adler with you. He'll be able to know if Coleus surrenders the real records or not. Bevan says she doesn't trust Dr. Coleus. Apparently, he has quite a history."

Detective Swan added, "We've had a chance to interview several nurses who have worked with Dr. Coleus. Not one of them had a good thing to say about him."

"There was one older nurse who hinted that if we really wanted to know about Coleus, we need to track down a Lucy Spencer. She indicated that this Lucy was a nurse whom Coleus falsely blamed for the death of a patient on the operating table some time ago," Morrison stated. "I've put feelers out through the Nurse's Association trying to locate her."

Chapter 10

When Andrew entered the cafeteria for his dinner break, he noticed Nurse Rice sitting by herself over to the far side of the room. He began to get nervous. A single bead of sweat started to form on his forehead. At home, alone, in front of his mirror, he had practiced over and over again exactly what he was going to say. But now, knowing it was time, he couldn't remember any of the words he had practiced. As he approached Nurse Rice's table, the single bead of sweat on his forehead, was joined by others.

"Nurse Rice," his voice cracked from his dry throat.

Michele looked up. Seeing it was the orderly, Andrew, she jokingly said, "You're going to have to put a bell on yourself to warn people when you're sneaking up on them."

Andrew didn't understand the joke and couldn't figure out if Nurse Rice was making fun of him or not. Maybe this was a bad idea, he thought to himself.

Michele could tell that Andrew was nervous about something. In an attempt to put him at ease, "Andrew, would you like to join me?" she offered.

This was too good to be true. Andrew now knew she had to be making fun of him. Why had he attempted to do this today, he thought to himself. He wasn't ready and it was turning out all wrong.

Pulling a chair out, "Here, it's alright. Sit down. I have a few minutes before I have to go back," Michele said.

Her warm smile, started to ease the tension he was feeling. He sat down, but never said a word.

This is an awfully strange man, Michele thought to herself. But when she looked at him, in some quirky way she felt an attraction to him. Maybe it was his total innocence, or maybe it was his innocence combined with his cuddly appearance that she felt. Michele didn't know, but she knew something was there.

"How's your night going so far?" Michele asked, in an attempt to try to break the awkward silence.

"Alright, I guess," he struggled to answer with his throat now dry as dust.

Michele kept looking at him. What was it about this man? It wasn't love or any remote type of romance, but there was something, and try as she might, she just couldn't put her finger on it.

With supreme effort, "Are you married?" Andrew blurted out. Asking the question gave him a surprising feeling of calm. He had done it. He had jumped over the first hurdle of fear.

Hearing the question delivered in such an abrupt manner startled Michele. It took her a moment to recover, "That's rather a personal question, Andrew. Why would you ask it?"

"I need to know. That's all," he replied with his head hung down as he waited for her to answer. To Andrew, everything depended on how she answered. If she was married, then it was over. He would never attempt to impose himself between a wife and her husband. Thoughts of his mother and her husbands would never allow it. But, if she wasn't married, then there was a chance for him.

Michele sat back in her chair. Was she married? That was a hell of a question to come out of this man. Then she thought, maybe that was it. Andrew, in his simple straight forward way wasn't really a man at all. He wasn't capable of the lies, the deceit of normal men. He was a child, unspoiled by the way of men. "No, I'm not married. I was once, but that was just a foolish mistake I had made a long time ago."

Andrew's face lit up with a broad grin of happiness, "Do you like red wine?"

The questions Andrew was asking were causing Michele to have a series of flash back memories. She remembered a time when she thought her life would have days filled with sitting in the sun, on a patio, sipping a glass of smooth red wine as she watched the world parade pass in front of her.

“It’s been a long time since I’ve had any red wine,” she answered wishfully.

“I like red wine,” Andrew said, his voice filled with hope.

*****

Michele lay in her bed and stared at the ever-increasing ceiling crack above her. She wasn’t sure how this evening had gotten so out of control. At the bottom of her bed, her two cats gave her angry looks. Their place in the bed had been taken over by a pudgy young man who slept away while gurgling sounds rose from his open mouth.

When Andrew had asked her, in his awkward way, if she was a good cook, what else could she say. In the early days of her marriage to Mario, she cooked up a storm. When he would come home from his day out, there was always a hot, delicious meal waiting for him. She prided herself in knowing the old phrase, ‘*The way to a Man’s Heart was through his stomach.*’ She had worked hard to prepare meals with just the right amount of spice to both satisfy and tantalize her man. And after the meal, Mario would always satisfy her. Their love making would often go well into the evening.

The early days of her marriage were wonderful. But that had all changed quickly. It changed when she learned what her husband, Mario, actually did on his days out. At first, she thought he had a wonderful job. There appeared to always be more than enough money for her to buy the things that she wanted and needed. Then the money started to get less and less. And when she saw the bank accounts steadily drain till there was nothing left, she realized Mario had made a fool of her. With no money left for him to spend on his wild schemes, he up and left her and the cooking stopped.

So, when Andrew asked her, she thought it might be nice, to cook once again. Yes, she told him, she was a wonderful cook. Then when he asked her with such a soft timid voice that she felt reach down and pull at her heart, if she would cook a meal for him like his mother used to cook, how could she refuse. There was just something about the innocent, unspoiled, boy-like qualities of Andrew that kept drawing her to him. She agreed she would cook a delicious meal for him on her next day off. At the time, she had thought it would be harmless and might actually brighten up one of her drab evenings that she normally would spend alone, locked in her apartment with her cats.

She spent her day off shopping for food. There was nothing in her apartment. She hadn't really cooked in a long, long time. All she had was some food for her cats and some quick ready made food to microwave for herself. As she shopped and picked up the food and spices she remembered using, a genuine excitement started to take hold of her. Sampling this and tasting that, she searched for just the right ingredients to bring life to her dull, small kitchen. When she had everything she needed, she hurried back to her apartment to begin the transformation. These ingredients would be mixed, blended, toasted and cooked till a meal that would have made Julia Child envious had been prepared. Her shopping spree had cost her a lot, far more than she had originally planned to spend, and far more than she could really afford. She couldn't stop herself and the joy she was feeling was worth it.

With the food ready, she hurriedly cleaned herself up. In her closet she pulled out her one and only good dress that she had saved from her marriage. A dress that showed off her long legs in enticing detail. She had been saving it in the oft chance she ever met her Prince Charming. What the hell, who was she kidding, she thought to herself. There was never going to be a Prince Charming coming for her. What was the point of saving anything. Andrew was a long way from any Prince Charming, but tonight, it wasn't about Andrew. It was about her. She wanted to feel good about herself again. The type of feeling she felt long ago and had wasted so much time waiting for it to return.

When the knock on her door came, she was ready. The apartment had been cleaned. She had even attempted, with limited success, to vacuum the cat hair from her couch. The food was ready and filled the apartment with a warm aroma. And most important, she was ready. A quick glance in her mirror showed an amazing woman that had been hidden away for far too long.

She opened her door to find Andrew standing there holding a large bottle of what appeared to be cheap red wine. At first, she was disappointed. She didn't know quite what she had expected, but Andrew stood there wearing the same clothes he always wore. Clothes that you would wear if you were taking your dog for a walk or if you had to run out to the drug store in the middle of the night for some cough medicine. Maybe he could have at least worn a shirt that had a button-down collar or a sports jacket that would have given him a more hip, with it look.

"I've brought some wine," Andrew said cheerfully. "I thought we could do some toasting later. My mother and I always toasted with red wine after dinner."

It was there. That child like, unspoiled innocence, that made everything alright. "I'm glad you've come," Michele said. "Come in quickly before the cats slip out."

Andrew entered. He went to the living area and planted himself on the couch. He took a moment and looked around. With him living in his spacious mother's house, this apartment seemed small, even to him. "You live here?" he asked.

"I know it's small, but with just me and my two cats it's all I need. You get used to its size." Michele lied;

she dreaded her apartment. It was small, dull and in need of repair, but it was all she could afford.

"I guess so," Andrew answered. "Your cats are nice." Mr. Briggs had climbed up and settled himself in Andrew's lap and began to purr loudly as Andrew started rubbing the cat's head.

"Dinner's all ready. Just push him to the side and come into the kitchen. We want to eat while the dinner's still hot."

Despite the minor disappointment caused by Andrew's clothes, Michele was having a wonderful time. She enjoyed as she played 'Hostess', jumping up to get this and moving to serve that. It was a pleasant evening. For dessert, she had prepared the '*Piece de Resistance.*' It was a light fluffy cake smothered with a rich creamy chocolate sauce. It had been a long time since Andrew had eaten so well. Eagerly he had been stuffing everything that Michele placed in front of him, into his mouth. There seemed to be no end to how much he could eat.

With the dinner finally over and with Andrew completely stuffed, Michele rose to begin the clean up process.

"Can we have some wine now?" Andrew asked expectantly. "I brought the wine so we could make our toasts."

Michele, with her focus on the dinner meal, had forgotten all about Andrew and his wine. "Of course," she apologized. "Here let me get some glasses." She had no proper wine glasses. All she had was a couple of plastic water tumblers that she used daily. "I guess these will have to do," she informed Andrew. He didn't mind, he was anxious to start making toasts. He had been thinking all day about the toast he would make. He filled the water tumblers. In his excitement he filled them both right to the brim.

"You first," he said. "My mother always made the first toast."

Michele took her tumbler and raised it. "To good health," she toasted and took her first sip of the red wine. It had been a long time since she had tasted any wine, and the warmth of this wine surprised her.

"Now me," Andrew stated. "I toast to all the people at our hospital who we help everyday." Michele was taken back by the sincerity of the toast that Andrew had given. She never expected such a thoughtful sentiment from him. She took another sip from her tumbler.

"No, no," Andrew declared. "With the toast you have to drink all your wine."

Michele looked at her tumbler, "That's a lot of wine to be drinking."

"You have to or the toast doesn't become real," he pleaded.

When Michele looked at Andrew and saw the expectation in his eyes, she didn't want to disappoint him. She raised the tumbler to her lips and with a couple of gulps, downed the sweet liquid.

"Again, again," Andrew cried out, his voice full of joy.

The tumblers were filled and another round of toasts with the glass emptying ritual was completed.

Somewhere after downing three or four full tumblers of the potent mixture, Michele couldn't remember exactly how many, the large wine bottle was emptied. Maybe it was the combination of the wine in her belly, the heat from the tiny kitchen, the expectation of the dinner, and the feeling of happiness that had set in on her after being absent for so long; but here she was. In bed, naked, with a cuddly naked man sleeping peacefully beside her. She knew nothing had happened between the two. Andrew was far too drunk and had passed out as soon as his head had hit the pillow. She wasn't sure how she felt. Was she angry with herself that she let the evening get so out of control? Or was she angry with Andrew that nothing happened? All she could really do now, was to hope that the naked man-boy, sleeping in her bed, had been drunk enough that he wouldn't remember any of this by morning.

Chapter 11

He stood quietly at her open door and watched her, as she worked away at her desk, unaware that he was there. There was no question she was beautiful, that was never the issue. In her beauty there was an elegance that totally mesmerized him. Unable to control himself, he silently watched her hold her pen at just the right angle as her hand smoothly glided across the page on which she was writing. Her short auburn hair, with ever so slight traces of blond highlites, brushed teasingly against her forehead. Deep brown eyes shone with shimmers of gold in the stark florescent light of her office. He couldn't help but wonder if he had made the right decision by pushing her away. Why was it so important that he had to feel freedom? Why had he sacrificed his chance at love just so he could have his own way? A feeling of doubt crept over him. Had he made a mistake, a terrible, terrible mistake?

"Jason," she said surprised when she finally looked up and saw him. "How long have you been standing there?"

"For just a minute," he answered. "You looked so intense that I didn't want to disturb you." As he stood there watching her, watching him, he could see a change sweep over her. Her cheeks flushed pink, the gold in her eyes sparkled, the corners of her full lips moved upwards in a smile that couldn't be denied. Oh God, he thought to himself. Her overwhelming beauty was far too powerful. It was clear to him now, pushing her away had been a mistake!

When he had seen her in Dr. Bevan's office, he was able to control himself. In the presence of the Doctor, he always had his guard up. He knew Bevan had her fantasies about him, but he had made it a point to always hold a professional distance from her. But here, now, looking at Claire, after being apart for so long, he wanted no distance between them. He wanted to move across the office, take her in his arms, feel her warm body mould to his and taste the sweetness of her lips.

"Well don't just stand there," she beckoned. "Come in and sit down."

The closer he moved towards her, the more he couldn't take his eyes off of her. The pink flush of her cheeks had begun to turn to red. And now he could smell her.

The scent from her surrounded him carrying the slightest hint of the freshness of spring.

“What brings you all the way over here?” she asked.

He had to pull himself together. It was either that or he’d have to close and lock her door.

Outside the office, Detective Morrison watched in fascination. Seeing the two, and the obvious heat they were giving off, brought back memories of he and his wife. Memories of the love dance they performed every time they came near each other, in the years before they had their three boys. Tony picked up his phone, he wanted to send his wife, Carol, flowers, with a little note attached, *‘You and Me forever.’*

“Since we are going to be working closely together on the St. Luke’s Hospital matter, I thought we should talk,” Jason stated.

Claire said nothing. She wanted to wait and see where Jason was going with his *‘talk.’* Was it going to be all business, or was it going to be personal?

Through the corner of his eye, Jason could see Detective Morrison watching them, and he felt strangely uncomfortable and guilty. “Do you think we could step out for a coffee?” With a nod towards the Detective, “There’s too many prying eyes here.”

So, it is going to be personal, Claire thought to herself. "There's a coffee shop just around the corner," she offered.

As they passed by Morrison's desk, Claire said, "I'll be out for a couple of minutes. "I'm sure you've got some work you should be doing."

*****

Jason Adler, along with Detectives Julian Swan and Tony Morrison sat quietly in the office of Dr. Mark Coleus. They were waiting for the doctor to return from doing his early morning rounds. The three would have waited in the Doctor's outer office had there been a receptionist there. Since no one was present to stop them, they decided to show the Doctor who was in charge by occupying his office.

It was taking Coleus longer to complete his rounds this morning. He had needed to inform the Lead Nurse on each floor that the hospital's computer system had been compromised and that they should not give any medicines to any of his patients, no matter what the computer said, without first checking with him personally. It was a nuisance having to talk to each of them, but the Harris incident had unnerved him. He didn't know how his account had been hacked, but until the hospital's IT Department improved the computer security system, he had no choice.

"Why are you in my office?" Coleus challenged the police detectives when he finally was able to return. "You have no right to just barge in anytime you feel like it. I've a good mind to report this to your superiors." Without saying a word, both Julian and Tony looked to Jason. "And who have you brought with you this time?" Coleus asked when he saw the extra man the two police detectives had turned to.

Jason never flinched at the bravado displayed by the doctor. With a calm voice, a voice that carried with it the tone of someone who knew the power he held, "Good morning, Dr. Coleus. My name is Jason Adler and I am the senior investigator for Dr. Marianne Bevan, the County Medical Examiner."

Coleus had never heard of Jason Adler, but he was well aware of Dr. Bevan. She had been a thorn in his side several times in the past. To have both the police and the front man for Dr. Bevan in his office, at the same time, wasn't good. His attitude quickly changed from being indignant to one of being cautious. With all that had been going on around him lately, he felt he was in no position to attempt to match wits with the Medical Examiner's Office.

"This morning, we served a 'Notice to Comply' to your hospital's legal department and thought you'd appreciate it if we personally stopped by to give you your copy of the Medical Examiner's Order," Jason said with his voice dripping with sarcasm. He rose from his chair and walked over to stand directly in front of Coleus. As he stared squarely in the doctor's eye, without so much as a blink, he slapped the white envelope into the doctor's hand. "You can read it if you like, but it directs you to immediately surrender any and all medical records you have concerning Mr. Henry Bittman."

Coleus thought for a moment. If they were only interested in Bittman, then they were only at the tip of the iceberg. He could handle the 'Bittman' issue. If he did it right, he was confidant he could stop any further investigation into his ongoing 'Death Angel' problem that was plaguing the hospital. His first step, he thought, would be to make sure they weren't bluffing. He had heard of people spilling their guts out to the police when they were threatened with a bluff.

"I'll need to check with our legal department first, if you don't mind," he said. He watched the three for any tell-tale reaction that would tip their hand. As he looked to Adler, a crazy thought ran through his mind. '*This man never blinked*!' Jason's stare never wavered from being locked onto the doctor. It was unnatural and more than a little freaky to him.

"Yes, yes," Coleus said into his phone. "You're sure. Yes, they're here in my office now." He listened. "She has that authority?" he asked. "But what about my rights and those of my patients?" He listened. "Alright, if you say so," he hung up the phone abruptly.

Jason looked to the two detectives and gave them his '*I told you so*' smile.

"Our legal department tells me they have already forwarded all of the Bittman records to the Medical Examiner's Office," Coleus told the trio. "But I feel I should inform you that the records may not be accurate."

Coleus could see that this statement had hit a nerve. For the first time he saw Adler blink. "Recently the hospital's computer system has been hacked. Why, would you believe it. Whoever was responsible even altered some of my medical orders. Of course, I immediately informed our IT department, but there's no telling what other records they might have altered." The sly grin Coleus had on his face made Jason's face turn cold. Jason knew the doctor had just given himself an escape card.

Chapter 12

"Where are we with the 'Bittman' case?" Claire asked her two detectives. "The Commissioner's been pressuring me for a report on any of the progress we've made so far."

Tony pulled out his note pad and began to read, "Dr. Coleus has been served with the 'Order to Comply' that had been drawn up by the Medical Examiner, Dr. Bevan. I believe her and Adler are going through the medical reports they were given, even as we speak."

"But there's a bit of a hic-up," Julian stated.

"What do you mean hic-up?" Claire asked.

"Well, as I understand it," Julian continued. "Recently the hospital computer system had been hacked. And Adler was concerned that even if they find anything in Bittman's medical records, Coleus could claim it was a result of some unknown hacker."

"Damn it," Claire cursed. "So we're no farther ahead than we were. All we have is a number of well minded people thinking somethings going on with absolutely no real solid evidence."

"That's about the size of it," both her detectives agreed.

"What about Coleus's financial records. To my knowledge there's been no hacker activity on the bank's computer," she said sarcastically.

"Hold on," Detective Swan responded. "Don't start taking your frustration out on us."

The Sergeant looked at Swan and knew that he was right. It wasn't their fault that at first she hadn't taken the 'Bittman' letter seriously. It was her fault. But that was in the past. After listening to Dr. Bevan, she now believed Bittman had been murdered. And chances were high, with the possibility of a serial killer operating freely inside the hospital, there were more murders yet to be discovered.

"To answer your question," Detective Morrison answered. "We're still waiting for the District Attorney's Office to give us the signed court order."

Claire picked up her phone, "Mona," she said when her department clerk answered. "Get after the DA's office and get me that order for the financial statements of Dr. Coleus." She listened. "No, I don't care what their problem is. I need that order now," she said then hung up the phone without waiting for any reply.

"The minute we get the paper work, I want those financials gone over with a fine-tooth comb. We need to know everything we can about this doctor. Now what about this nurse you were looking for?"

"You mean Lucy Spencer. I've found her. We're scheduled to meet with her this afternoon," Tony stated. "When I talked to her on the phone and mentioned we wanted to speak to her about Dr. Coleus, she couldn't wait to get together with us."

"Remember when you interview her to get the names of anyone who can collaborate her statements. Without that collaboration, all we'll have is her word against Coleus's," Claire warned.

*****

The two detectives huddled in the back booth of the coffee shop and tried to look as inconspicuous as they could. But it didn't work. They might as well have hung a neon light above the booth, flashing '*Cops Sitting Here.*' The young patrons, lounging about, drinking their Cappuccinos and Mocha Lattes, as they played on their laptops and phones, knew exactly who the two in the back booth were.

"What time did she say she'd be here?" Swan asked impatiently.

Morrison glanced at his watch, “Any time now.”

Julian squirmed in his seat, as he hunted to find a comfortable spot. “I think they make these booths small on purpose. And whatever this ‘Mocha Hell’ is that I’m drinking, it tastes like crap.”

“Stop your complaining,” his partner chuckled. “She’ll be here.”

The shop door opened. The little bell ‘*tinkled*’ and Lucy Spencer stood in the doorway. It took a moment, till her eyes adjusted to the dim light of the place, to spot the detectives.

“Which one of you is Detective Morrison,” she asked.

“That’s me,” Tony answered as he scuched over so the woman could sit down. “And this is my partner, Detective Swan.”

Lucy gave an acknowledging nod towards Julian. As she slid into the booth, she plopped her oversized black bag onto the table in front of her.

Julian eyed the woman. He was sure her bag weighed more than she could possibly have weighed. Her hair, obviously dyed red, he thought, was cut short. The dark, wrinkled weathering of her skin, from bouts of heavy smoking, made her appear much older than she probably was.

"I want to thank you for agreeing to meet with us," Tony started.

Lucy jumped right to the point. "It's about time you people locked up that incompetent bastard. He's gotten away with murder for far too long."

Swan looked to his partner with his eyes opened a little bit. There was no nicety about this woman. She was going right for the throat.

"Can we back up a little bit?" Tony asked. "Let's take a minute and start from the beginning if you wouldn't mind."

"Humpt," Lucy said.

"When did you first meet Dr. Coleus?"

"I remember it as if it was yesterday," she began. She told her tale straight through, while hardly stopping to take a breath.

Tony wrote furiously as he tried to keep up to the tirade spewing from the woman's lips.

"Hold on, so I get this right," Tony said. "The other doctor in the operating room was a Dr. Turner?" He remembered what his Sergeant had told him about getting names of witnesses who could collaborate the woman's statement.

"Yes, Dr. Turner, the anesthetist," Lucy responded, clearly annoyed that the detective had interrupted her. "Turner was right. He warned me to keep an eye on Coleus," she said as she shook her head.

"And you say that Dr. Coleus mistakenly cut the wrong artery and the patient bled to death?"

"Yes. The damn fool was more interested in getting to his golf game on time, than he was in watching what he was doing. He murdered that man!"

Detective Swan had been listening to every word the woman had said. "If it's as you say, at best it's a case of Medical Malpractice. I wouldn't call it murder."

Lucy turned to Swan, her eyes throwing fire at the detective. "You tell that to the widow, Mary Brompton and her six-year-old son. I tell you Coleus murdered Darel Brompton."

'*Brompton, Brompton.*' Tony had heard that name before. Just recently it had come up. He sat thinking, wracking his brain as he tried to remember where he had heard it. He could no longer hear Lucy as she continued to rattle on. Where had he heard it? '*Brompton, Brompton.*' Round and round the name swirled in his brain, with no luck. It just wouldn't come to him. He took his pencil and drew a dark circle around the name in his notebook. As soon as he saw the name inside the circle it came to him. That was the name he had circled before. Andrew Brompton, the hospital orderly Nurse Rice claimed was on duty the night Henry Bittman died.

Tony looked directly at Lucy. "You're absolutely certain that the patient you claim Dr. Coleus murdered was Darel Brompton?"

"Of course it was Darel Brompton. I should know. Coleus ruined my career. That's not something you easily forget."

"And the other doctor, Turner. He can collaborate everything you've said?"

Swan could see the wheels spinning in his partner's eyes. He was on to something. Swan didn't know what, but by the way Tony was attempting to nail down the facts, it must be good.

"Thank you, Ms. Spencer. If there's anything else, we know how to get hold of you," Tony announced. He was done talking to this woman, with her endless ranting. With the name 'Brompton' top of his mind, he had work to do.

*****

In the car, as the two detectives made their way back to the station, Swan waited. He could see his partner had one of his stupid grins plastered from one side of his face to the other.

"Well, are you going to let me in on it?"

"In on what?" Tony played with his partner.

"Don't give me that. If you grinned anymore, I'd have to put sunglasses on," Swan stated. "Something that crazy woman said triggered something in you. Now what was it?"

Tony couldn't help himself; he was feeling so good. "Didn't you hear it?"

Julian was starting to get annoyed. "Now cut it out. What was it?" he demanded.

"Darel Brompton," Tony replied. "Darel Brompton and his six-year-old son."

That meant absolutely nothing to Julian. "Yeah, Darel Brompton was the patient that died on the operating table. That was twenty some odd years ago. What's that got to do with anything. You and I both know attempting to chase Medical Malpractice that might have happened twenty years in the past is a waste of time."

"Don't you see? It all fits. It's not the dead father, it's the son. Andrew Brompton was the orderly on duty the night 'Bittman' was murdered. He is the orderly that Nurse Rice claimed liked to sit alone, supposedly talking to patients in their rooms. Andrew Brompton is getting even with Coleus for killing his father. Andrew Brompton killed Bittman!"

"Jesus," Swan exclaimed. "And we didn't even think enough to interview him."

Chapter 13

Dr. Bevan sat hunched over her desk as she stared at her computer screen. This was the third time she had read over the Medical Records that her office had received from St. Luke's Hospital. At first glance, the records appeared to fulfill her '*Order to Comply*' that she had issued to the hospital. They were the medical records of Henry Bittman, she was sure of that, but to her trained eye, there was an awful lot missing. The records detailed the Angioplasty procedure Dr. Coleus had performed on Bittman. Coleus had inserted a stent by means of a catheter incision into the patient's groin with no indication of there being any problem. The recorded vital signs taken by nurses over the next couple of hours were all remarkably good. Blood pressure was stable, temperature was normal, indicating no infection was present and the heartbeat was strong and regular. The records showed everything Bevan expected to see from a middle aged, healthy man. It was what the records didn't show that concerned her. They had omitted anything about the patient's sudden death. All they showed was that at 3:15am the patient experienced a major heart occurrence that resulted in death. The death was declared by a Dr. Fletcher.

"Marjorie," the doctor called out to her assistant. "Can you tell Jason I want to see him."

When Adler arrived at her office, he could tell that his boss was uneasy about something. There was no sparkle in her eye or silly grin across her face that she normally had whenever she saw him. Instead, her face was cold and her eyes were focused on nothing, as she stared blankly out into space. She had drifted into deep, deep thought.

"Ah-hum," Jason cleared his throat to tell the doctor that he was there. She never responded. Her thoughts had a hold of her and wouldn't let her go.

"Dr. Bevan," Jason announced as he tried again. "You wanted to see me?"

The doctor just waved her hand towards one of her office chairs as she continued to think. Jason sat down and quietly waited. Still the doctor sat motionless, oblivious to her surroundings.

"I'm sorry," she said when she finally came around. "Coleus is hiding something," she said point blank. She then proceeded to go though her line of thought with her investigator. "You can see here with these records we received," she started. " … , but when it comes to the death, there is nothing."

"What had you expected to see?" Jason asked the woman. "When I read over them, they detail a successful procedure that later resulted in a death. That sounds all possible to me."

"No, no, no," Bevan replied in frustration, banging her clenched fist on her desk. "You're missing it." Bevan couldn't believe her senior investigator had missed what was obvious to her. She remembered that he had also missed the presence of a 'Death Angel', that she had detected, when he had read the Mortality Reports. "What's got into you lately? You're behaving like a junior employee," she chided. "I expect far better from you. Your performance lately is totally unacceptable. Now whatever your problem is, you better get your head in the game. We have very serious events going on over at St. Luke's that demand our very best skills."

Jason was taken aback. He hadn't expected to receive this type of rebuke from the doctor. Normally she always treated him with kid gloves, and often outright flirted with him. Now she was taking her heavy boots and walking up one side of him and straight down the other. Sure, he thought to himself. He had been overly caught up with his relationship with Claire. His love life with the Sergeant had been on a rocky road. During his recent heart to heart with Claire at the coffee shop, they had spent time going over their, or should he admit it, his problems. They had worked everything out and in fact were discussing the two of them going away alone for a couple of days. Days when they could fully rekindle the love that he had damaged. The kiss they had when they left to return to work was warm and loving. It told of a hunger they missed and a commitment for a future. But that all had to wait, they agreed, until the 'Bittman' and St. Luke's issues were resolved. After a moment of thought, he wasn't sure if he deserved the tongue lashing the doctor had given him. Had his job performance suffered or was the doctor jealous of his renewed happiness with Claire Reindle? Jason decided he had better keep his mouth shut for now.

*****

"And you're sure of this?" the Sergeant asked.

"We did as you suggested and contacted the other doctor that was in the operating room that day," Detective Morrison affirmed. "He collaborated with everything Spencer had told us."

"Yeah, a Dr. Turner," Detective Swan added. Swan wanted to make sure he was part of the discussion. "Turner moved out of the area shortly after the incident."

"Alright then," Claire directed. "I don't want to make any move on our suspect, Andrew Brompton, just yet. First, I want you to arrange to bring this Lucy Spencer in to make a formal statement. Make sure the statement clearly states the events and most important the name of the patient. We need to have everything buttoned up tight, with no loose ends. All we have here is the motive for the killing of Bittman. It's a start, but it's not enough to get a murder conviction."

"Bringing the Spencer woman in will be easy to do. She's so filled with hate, she'll do anything if she thinks we're going after Coleus," Detective Morrison stated.

"Are we going after Coleus?" Julian was confused with what his partner had said. "Who are we going after? The orderly or the doctor?"

"Our job is to go after the 'Bittman' killer," the Sergeant said. "There's plenty of time for Coleus later. Don't worry, I'm going to be talking with the Medical Examiner, Dr. Bevan, about what to do with Coleus."

*****

Dr. Bevan was pleased with herself. She had stood her ground and she wasn't about to let anyone, especially Sergeant Reindle, push her around. When Claire had attempted to coerce her to travel over to the Police Services Building, she wanted no part of that. She didn't like driving and the traffic around the building always made her nervous. She had examined more than enough traffic accident victims on her autopsy table and had no intention to have her body added to the mix. If the Sergeant wanted to see her, let her be the one to fight the traffic.

"With the 'Bittman' medical records we received from St. Luke's I believe I have more than enough material to have the State Medical Board, levy sanctions against Dr. Coleus," Bevan stated.

“What material do you have? When I read the records, I didn’t see anything,” Claire asked.

It didn’t surprise the doctor. She had jealously determined that both her Investigator and this Sergeant were so caught up in themselves that they were having difficulties focusing on their jobs. It was time to give this girl a lesson.

“What you didn’t see is what is important and missing from those medical records. State law dictates that any death that occurs in a hospital setting within 24 hours of a medical procedure must be immediately reported to the Medical Examiner of the region. The body must be held intact until the Medical Examiner’s Office decides if an autopsy is warranted. An autopsy would be performed to determine if the death was due to Medical Malpractice, an Illegal Act, or Natural Causes. Unfortunately, none of this was done. The Bittman body was released to a Funeral Home and a cremation took place before my office was notified.” Dr. Bevan made a point of staring down on the Sergeant. “Do you understand now?”

Claire didn’t like the tone that the doctor was using, but she was in no position to get into a *‘discussion’* with her. She had to bite her tongue. She needed the doctor’s help.

“So, if I understand it,” Claire said. “You are in no position to declare Bittman died due to an illegal act? I have a suspect who was in the area that night and who we believe has a solid motive to commit murder as an act of revenge against Dr. Coleus. But, without your declaration I can't prove a murder was committed."

"Ah, not necessarily so," the Doctor replied with a wry grin. "I plan to use the pressure of the sanctions against our Dr. Coleus to have him declare the cause of death. As the doctor on record, his word would carry the weight we need to state a murder was committed."

Claire sat back. That's okay for now she thought. But when this is all over, you and I are going to talk, old woman!

*****

"You want to be on your guard," Michele's work partner warned her. "I've heard rumours from some of the other nurses working the night shift, about that crazy cat woman, Doris. Apparently, she's been coming into work, late at night, to check up on the nurses who were working."

Doris Hopkins, sat alone in her dark office. With just her small desk lamp on, it provided an eerie glow across her two cat pictures. When she looked at the picture of the overweight black cat, that was stretched out across her hair covered couch, she frowned. She always frowned when she looked at that picture. It had been '*His*' cat. The cat that had been just like he had been, an overweight, lying around, lazy bully. The cat that he had named '*Sampson*', after himself, he had told her. What a joke! Neither Jim, nor the cat, were anything like a '*Sampson*'. The Sampson she knew of, from her bible tales, was a gorgeous man, covered with rippling muscles with long vibrant hair that shone with the rich blackness of night. The real Sampson wasn't anything like the fat bald man who lounged on her couch, day after day.

When she had turned fifty, she had become deeply depressed. None of her dreams had come true. She hadn't experienced the wonders of love, of marriage or of children and she suddenly realized she had nothing to show for any of it. She had been a workaholic nurse now three quarters of the way through her life.

A friend of hers had introduced her to Jim. Even then he was nothing to look at. But in her depressed state she had latched on to him. At the time, she thought he was better than nothing, and besides, as her friend had told her, '*There's no one else beating a path to your door!*' Having a man in her life cheered her up. She looked upon Jim as a challenge. Despite what he was, she really felt she could change him and mold him into a man she could be proud of. In her life, she had rarely failed at anything, but she certainly failed with Jim. He had turned out to be a mean, ugly, bully.
Whenever she had suggested anything that she hoped would make even the smallest of an improvement in him, Jim had lashed out in furious anger. She had often gone into work with claims of having fallen or mistakenly run into a door. She knew everyone at work knew the truth. She could hear them talking

behind her back '*... poor Doris. ... did you see the bruises on her today? ... I don't know how she puts up with it ...*' She had lost all trace of the confidence and dignity that she once had. Her downward spiral had her sneaking around work, as she tried not to be seen by anyone.

But fate, wonderful, glorious fate finally swung her way. In the midst of a fit of rage, Jim's red face had turned purple. His jaw had clamped shut. He grabbed at his chest as he fell to the floor with a thud. Doris knew what was happening. She had been a nurse long enough to know all the signs. Jim was in the middle of suffering a major heart attack. She knew what she was supposed to do, what she had been trained to do, but she did nothing. She watched as he squirmed at her feet. His eyes bulged. Sweat covered him. He gurgled as he tried to plead with her for help. She did absolutely nothing. She stared at him, smiled at him and waited.

When the end came, it was as if the brightness of the sun had finally broken through the dark clouds that had engulfed her. With Jim gone from her life, there was only one more thing she had to do. She picked up the black cat, 'Sampson', his cat, and took it to her bathroom. As the last act of achieving release from the darkness of pain, she proved that cats really couldn't swim.

Tonight, she had returned to her office to do some unannounced checkups of the night time nurses. She had scanned through her computer and read the latest 'End of Shift' nursing reports that had been posted. Once satisfied that she had seen all she needed to see, she turned off her desk lamp and left her office. She had work that needed to be done.

Chapter 14

Claire called out to her detectives, “Morrison, Swan, get in here.” She had just returned from her meeting with Dr. Bevan and was anxious to follow up on what she had learned. Under pressure from Dr. Bevan, Dr. Coleus had no choice but to declare the Bittman death as suspicious. The Bittman investigation could now finally move from chasing a widow’s grief letter to chasing an active killer.

“What have you done about this orderly Brompton?” she asked.

“He’s scheduled to come in for interviewing this afternoon.” Morrison replied.

“Well, lean on him,” she ordered. “With the right questions you might just trick him into making a mistake. You never know,” she pondered, “ a mistake now could lead to a confession later.”

*****

Andrew looked at the summons the uniformed policeman handed him. "I don't understand," he told the officer. "What does this mean?"

By the troubled look on Andrew's face, the officer could tell that this young man needed help. "What this summons says is that you are to report to the Main Police Station, today at 1:30, for an interview."

Andrew had never dealt with the police before and he couldn't figure out why anyone at the police department would want to interview him. "Have I done something wrong?" he asked. All he could think of was that the police were after him for being in bed with Nurse Rice. "I never meant to sleep in Nurse Rice's bed. We were only having a dinner and we drank some wine. When I woke up, I was in her bed," he tried to explain.

"I don't know what the detectives want to speak to you about. I only know that you need to be at the station by 1:30 or they will issue an arrest warrant for you."

Andrew's eyes sprung open, his jaw dropped, "But I didn't do anything. Nurse Rice is my friend," he insisted.

"Just make sure you're there," the officer said over his shoulder as he turned to leave.

*****

Andrew arrived early at the police station. The warmth of the afternoon sun did little to ease the worry that he felt. He had left his house in plenty of time since he had to take the Number 3 bus down to River Street, then transfer to the Main Cross Town bus to get there.

Once inside the heavy front door, it took him a moment to gather his bearings. Spread out directly in front of him, there was a large, encased counter, with a little window in the center.

Not knowing quite what to do, he handed the summons he had been given to the woman behind the glass and waited.

After having read the letter, “Are you Andrew Brompton?” she asked. When the woman spoke it was with the authority of one who was used to being obeyed.

“Yes,” Andrew replied meekly.

“You’ll have to speak up. I can’t hear you.”

“Yes,” Andrew shouted. He stood stiff. His eyes were bulged wide open as he waited for the woman to tell him what to do. He could feel an urgent urge to run and hide rapidly building up inside of him.

The woman took her time as she eyed Andrew up and down. Classifying him as a ‘Non-Threat’, “Sit in one of those chairs,” she ordered. “When you hear your name called, go to the screening station at the end of the hall." Her directions were clear and concise. She left no room for any questions to be asked.

Andrew had barely sat down when a cracked loudspeaker, located directly above his head, blared out his name. He wasn't sure if that was his name he heard. Again, the squawk filled the room. Looking around, he realized he was the only one sitting there. It had to be him they were calling, he thought. When he looked over towards the glassed-in woman for help, she just shook her head and pointed.

"Step inside the booth and raise your hands above your head," the uniformed officer directed with a dull, monotoned voice that was used to giving the same order over a hundred times each and every day.

Andrew did as he was told. He didn't know if anything was happening, he couldn't see or hear anything. He stood as still as he could with his hands stretched up high above his head.

"Alright, follow the officer; he'll escort you to your interview room."

Andrew really wished someone would tell him what was going on. All these officers with all these orders were making him very nervous. He kept trying to remind himself that he had done nothing wrong. This couldn't be because Nurse Rice complained he was in her bed. She was his friend.

*****

"You ready?" Tony asked his partner. "They just phoned to tell me he's sitting in Interview Room 2."

Julian looked at his watch, "He's early. Let him sit in there and sweat a bit first. Remember the Sarge said she wants a confession."

"Might as well have a coffee then while we wait. You want one?" Tony asked.

"Yeah, just a little cream. No sugar," he answered. "I've got my physical coming up," he said as he rubbed the bulge of his stomach.

After a good fifteen minutes of idle chit chat, Julian checked his watch again. "Okay, that should have him squirming by now."

Tony threw his head back and downed the last gulp of his black liquid, "Alright, I'm ready."

*****

Andrew couldn't believe the size of the two men when they entered the room. He had only seen men that big on TV when he watched Saturday Night Wrestling. Having them this close to him in such a small room, changed him from being nervous to being frightened. He had no idea what they had planned to do to him.

When Julian first saw Andrew, he couldn't keep himself from smiling. His waiting trick worked every time. By the look in this guy's eyes, Julian could tell he was terrified.

"Mr. Brompton," Tony began. "I'm Detective Tony Morrison and this is my partner Detective Julian Swan. I want to thank you for coming down to talk with us."

Andrew sat motionless, afraid to make any move.

"I have to inform you that everything we say is being recorded, so it's important for you to answer our questions as truthfully as you can. Do you understand?"

Andrew gave the slightest of nods with his head in response.

"I need you to answer," Det. Morrison stated.

Andrew took a gulp, "Yes."

Detective Swan began asking questions, one after another. "… was Andrew's father Darel Brompton …. Did Andrew work at St. Luke's Hospital … Did Andrew know Dr. Coleus … Did Andrew work nights …?" On and on the questions came.

It was all too much for Andrew. His eyes were frozen on the detective. He couldn't move. All he could manage to say was Yes, No, Yes, No. After a while he could no longer make out what the detective was asking. The questions kept coming. Yes, No. He'd say whatever they wanted him to say in the vain hope that they would stop.

Tony watched what was going on. He could see that Andrew had lost all contact with what was being asked and the answers that he was giving. This was no good, he had to do something. "I think we need to stop and take a break," he interrupted.

Julian shot a snap look at him in surprise. Tony returned the look with a subtle nod with his head towards the door. "We'll be back in a moment," he stated.

Outside in the hallway, Julian was beside himself. "What the hell did you do that for? Another couple of minutes I would have gotten a confession out of him."

"Another couple of minutes and you could have got him to admit to shooting Lincoln," Tony replied. "I don't think this kid's all there. There's no way we could use any of this in court."

"The Sergeant's not going to be pleased with you," Swan warned his partner.

"I can't help that; she can get as mad as she wants. There's no way we can continue. We need to get him mentally checked out before we go any further."

"Well, what do you suggest we do with him," Julian asked in a voice laced with disappointment. He had been on a winning streak and it bothered him to have it snatched away when he was so close to crossing the finishing line.

After thinking for a moment, "We might as well send him home. He's not going to go anywhere and we can't do anything with him here. If we keep him downstairs in one of the cells, who knows what trouble we'd catch from some smart-assed lawyer."

"You sure about this?" Julian asked.

"What choice do we have. If word got out that we knowingly locked up a mentally deficient suspect, it'd be our necks that would be in the noose, not his."

"Alright," Swan stated. He wanted a clear understanding with his partner of where the fault would fall when the Sergeant heard of their decision. "It'll be on you."

Tony gave a nod, "Yeah, I know."

*****

Nurse Rice, having just completed dishing out the evening meds to her patients, collapsed in her chair at the nursing station. "Now, if we're lucky, everyone will go to sleep and we'll have a quiet night," she said to her partner.

"I don't think there's much hope of that happening," her partner jokingly replied.

"No, I guess not," Michele sighed.

Michele had spent the first part of her shift, travelling the hallways, searching the patient rooms, hoping to find where the orderly, Andrew, was hiding out. She had not seen him since earlier that morning when he slipped out of her apartment before she had a chance to speak with him. No doubt, she thought, Andrew would be hung over and confused. She was worried about him. She needed to make sure he was okay.

Waking up, naked in bed, with an older woman beside him, would have been quite a traumatic experience for someone as innocent as Andrew. She also needed to make sure Andrew understood that what happened, was just an unfortunate turn of events. It wasn't his fault. She had let herself get carried away with her feelings of rediscovering the woman she had been. A woman who had been hidden away for such a long time. He needed to know that there was no romance or love involved. There was only an aging woman, unhappy with how her life had turned out, under the influence of a little too much wine, struggling to gain a moment of happiness.

Out of the corner of her eye she spotted the orderly, Andrew, coming down the hallway.

"Andrew," she called out to him. "Come over here, I need to talk with you."

Hearing his name, Andrew looked towards the nursing station to see it was the nice Nurse Rice that was calling him. In spite of the problems he now had because of waking up in bed beside her, he was eager to do anything he could for her. He knew his problems with the police weren't her fault. He had been bad and now he would have to accept his punishment. When he saw her, all he could think about was the tasteful meal she had made for him and the motherly toasts of wine she had shared with him. With a broad, childish grin showing on his chubby face, he hurried over to the nursing station. "Yes."

"Andrew, what are you doing right now?"

His grin quickly left his face and was replaced with a worried look. "Did I do something wrong?" he asked. "I'm supposed to be gathering up the empty gurneys to be returned to the Emergency Department. They told me I had to check every floor to find them."

"No, no," Michele reassured him. "You're fine. I just wanted to talk with you." Michele glanced around to make sure no one was within earshot. "Come on over here where no one will hear us," she directed.

"What about the gurneys I'm supposed to be gathering up? I don't want the people in emergency to be mad at me."

"Don't worry about that. I'll call them and tell them you're helping up here."

"I'm sorry," Andrew said sheepishly, with his head bowed so he didn't have to look Nurse Rice in her eyes.

"What are you sorry for?" Michele asked. She knew what had happened really had nothing to do with Andrew. "You have nothing to be sorry for. What happened last night was totally my fault. I shouldn't have let things get out of hand." She didn't want to try to explain her loneliness and her craving for a better life to this 'Boy'. "We need to put this behind us and pretend it never happened," she instructed. "Do you think you can do that?"

Andrew was confused. He didn't know what to think. "I know I've been bad. Sometimes I would climb into bed with my mother and she'd get really mad with me. She'd tell me that when you're a big boy, it's not right to be in a lady's bed. She told me that good boys always slept in their own bed with their pajamas on."

Michele half-heartedly felt sorry for Andrew. She realized she had nothing to fear from her mistake with him. It was clear to her that he wasn't looking for a relationship. At least not like the one in a normal way she so desperately wanted. This boy was looking for a mother.

"Your mother was right. Now we are both going to forget this ever happened," Michele said, glad to be able to put this mistake behind her.

Andrew nodded his head. "If you say so, I'll try."

Chapter 15

Buzz, buzz, buzz. The bell for Room 409 had started to ring again. Michele had been in the room three times already tonight. All three times she had rushed in, only to find there was nothing wrong. Mr. Blatchford just wanted to have someone to complain to. His bed was too lumpy. His pillow was too hard. He wanted his back rubbed. Michele had neither the time nor the patience to put up with Blatchford. It was bad enough she had to be slinging bedpans around most of the night, she wasn't here to be a babysitter.

Buzz, buzz, buzz, the bell continued to ring.

Lately Andrew had been spending all his free time hanging around Nurse Rice. With his problems from his recent talk with the two huge policemen he felt threatened. He knew he could trust Nurse Rice; she was so good to him. If anything more happened with the police, he was sure she would jump in and protect him. He tried his best to stay out of her way as she worked, but there was comfort being near her.

"I have a little bit of a problem that I think you can help me with," Michele started. She saw the familiar grin spread across his face.

"I'd be glad to do anything I can to help you."

"The patient in Rm 409, Mr. Blatchford, is being a real nuisance. He's constantly ringing his call bell and I don't have time to deal with him."

"What's wrong with him?"

Michele looked around to make sure no one could hear her, "He's had a stroke. There's no chance he's going to recover. His chart say's he will be bedridden for the rest of his life. He's just lonely and needs someone to sit and talk with him. Do you think you could do that for me? It would really help me a lot."

"Ok, if it will help you. That man really shouldn't be bothering you," Andrew declared. "I'll take care of it. He won't bother you anymore," he promised.

A short time later Andrew came back to the Nurse's Station with a glum look spread across his face. "I'm sorry, I don't think I've helped you.'"

Michele could see he felt rejected. "What do you mean?"

"I went to Rm 409 like you wanted, but the man was mean to me. He told me he didn't want me in his room. He wanted you. He called me names that I can't repeat to a lady."

"That's alright, at least you tried. After awhile he'll tire himself out and will go to sleep."

*****

Dr. Fletcher checked for any sign of life. The eyes had turned to glass. With his stethoscope he listened to the man's chest. There was no trace of any heart beat. The skin temperature had gone cold. With a glance towards the clock on the wall, "Record the time of death as 2:15am," he declared.

The nurse, who stood beside him, waited. "And what do I put down as the cause of death?" she asked.

Fletcher frowned, with a slow shake of his head, "I don't know!"

The nurse wrote 'Unknown' on the form. "At least Mr. Blatchford won't be a bother to the nurses anymore," she said half-heartedly.

Fletcher looked at her, surprised that she would say such an uncaring thing.

When Nurse Alice Franks arrived on the ward in the morning to begin her shift, she started by reading the night shift nurse's report. As she was reading the report, "Ahh, that's a shame."

"What is?" her partner asked.

"Mr. Blatchford, the stroke patient who was in Rm 409 passed away last night. It's funny but Dr. Fletcher declared cause of death as '*Unknown*'."

"I've been seeing more and more of that lately," her partner mused.

*****

"Dr. Bevan," Marjorie, her assistant, said. "There's a Dr. Fletcher on the phone. He says he works at St. Luke's Memorial Hospital and needs to speak with you."

Hmm, 'St. Luke's', Marianne thought. She was more than interested in talking to the Doctor.

"Put him on." She waited as she listened to the sounds of '*clicking*' from the phone lines being switched around. "This is Dr. Bevan," she said.

"Dr. Bevan, My name's Dr. Fletcher and I'm the night-time resident doctor at St. Luke's."

"Yes," Bevan replied. "And how can I help you?"

"I'm sorry to bother you so early this morning, but I have a situation that I'm feeling very uncomfortable about," Fletcher stated. He went on to explain the recent death that he had just certified earlier that night. " … the man had recently experienced a

'Cerebrovascular Incident'. Although his prognosis indicated the effects of the stroke were unrecoverable, he was stable. In fact, nurses had been recently indicating in their reports that he was a constant complainer."

Bevan listened to the Doctor. "Yes, I understand. So, what is this situation you say has made you uncomfortable?"

"It's just that," Fletcher started to fumble with his words. "I don't know quite how to explain it."

"Well give it a try," Bevan coached. She wanted, she needed, the doctor to formally tell her what she had already guessed he would say.

"I'm not sure if you're aware, but lately I have been finding an increasing number of unexplainable deaths here at St. Luke's. It's starting to really concern me. I can find no logical reason for Mr. Blatchford to suddenly die."

Dr. Bevan didn't want to admit that she had been tracking the rising number of deaths at the hospital, or that Dr. Coleus was thought to be at the center of the problem. "I want to thank you for your call. My office will immediately issue a '*Hold for Autopsy*' order for the remains of Mr. Blatchford. My assistant will arrange for the pick up and delivery of the body to our morgue here."

After Marianne had hung up from talking with Fletcher, she grinned to herself. Her premise of an active 'Death Angel' would no longer be just a feeling she had. Now, with the remains of one of the Angel's victims to work on, she would hopefully have solid proof.

"Marjorie, let me know the minute Blatchford is in our facility," she instructed her assistant. She debated whether she should inform her investigator, Adler or the Police Sergeant Reindle, of these latest developments. 'No' she thought, quite pleased with herself. It would be far better if she was the one who had the upper hand.

*****

Doris Hopkins lounged on her sofa with her bare feet dangling over the one end. Fresh from the shower, wrapped snuggly in her warm bathrobe, her mind had started to drift. Her orange tabby, craving the warmth, curled up in a tight ball on her lap. "I know," she murmured as she slowly patted the purring cat. "You miss Sampson, don't you? But I had no choice." The cat continued to purr, oblivious to the mournful ramblings of the woman. "You don't like living here alone, not having a partner to play with, do you?" Doris wasn't really talking to her cat; she was talking to herself. It was she who didn't like being alone. She was caught up in a world of 'What ifs'. What if Jim hadn't been so lazy? What if Jim hadn't been such a bully? What if Jim had been the man she had waited all her life for? What if he had loved her, truly loved her? The more she thought in her 'What if' world, the more she felt herself slipping down into her familiar depressed state. It wasn't fair. Everyone she worked with, all the nurses, all the doctors had loving relationships with someone. Some had a girl friend, a boyfriend, a husband, or a wife. Some even had children. How wonderful that would be to have the noise of children to fill her life instead of just a purring cat. She continued to stroke the cat and the cat continued to purr.

Jim! He could have changed everything. They would have had friends. Friends who would have come over for intimate dinner parties. Jim could have gone golfing in the afternoons with his work mates while she and the other wives could have gone shopping and spent idle time sipping on cool cups of sweet tea. She could have told tales of how well her boys, Tommy, Jimmy or maybe even Fred, who would have been named after her father, were doing in school. Possibly she could have bragged about her twin girls, Sandy and Mary, and tell of how well they were doing in their ballet classes. It could have all happened, except for Jim. The stroking that had started out as soft and tender turned hard and dug into the cat. '*Growl*' the cat screamed as it jumped to the floor. Doris watched as her cat walked away in disgust. This was all she had and now even her cat had abandoned her.

She glanced over towards her chiming wall clock. Nurse Michele Rice would just have started her work shift for tonight, she thought. A few nights ago, when she had slipped in unannounced to check up on how her nurses were doing, she had made it a point to check up on Nurse Rice. It was then that she had seen how the patient in Room 409 had been behaving so badly. She had watched as he had rung his call bell over and over again for no reason, continually interrupting Nurse Rice's important work. She had noticed when the orderly, Andrew, went into the patient's room in a feeble attempt to settle the patient down. It was a good thing, she realized, that she had chosen that night to go into the hospital for one of her checks, for that was the night Malcolm Blatchford passed away and her nurses could finally get on with their work.

Chapter 16

Dr. Bevan took her time as she donned her work scrubs. The baggy, pale blue scrubs were more than just her work clothes. When she put them on, they signified to her a sense of responsibility. With each piece of clothing, she had to move her mind from that of an accomplished doctor, teacher, lecturer to that of a hunter. These clothes changed her. She was no longer a woman. She couldn't allow her mind to stray from it's task. There would be no womanly thoughts of relationships or love to cloud her head. She knew she would need all of her mind and all of her skill to focus on the task that lay before her. She was about to travel on a journey through death. A journey both she and the cold body she was about to dissect, would take together, through the dark world of '*Man's Inhumanity to Man'*. She wasn't spiritual. The pain and suffering she had seen throughout her career, had washed that all away from her. She could only hope that through her efforts and her skill, she would arrive with some sense of peace at the end of the journey.

"We're ready for you, Doctor," the morgue assistant called to her. When she completed the final act of pulling on her protective booties, she was ready.

She took her place, directly in front of the gleaming stainless-steel table that held the body of Malcom Blatchford, with her assistant at her side.

"John, shave the head," she directed. "I'll be going into the cranial cavity to check the condition of the brain. The medical documents state that he experienced a severe, unrecoverable stroke. We'll need to rule that out as a possible cause of death."

John dutifully picked up the hair trimmer. With the gentle hum of the trimmer, he proceeded to clear away all trace of the thin gray hair, revealing the white skull cap that lay beneath.

Marianne gingerly picked up the razor-sharp scalpel from the equipment tray. "Okay, Mr. Blatchford. Let's see what you have to tell us." With skilled hands she sliced from the base of the neck all the way down to the naval. Then she made two cross cuts. One at the top and one at the bottom. Putting the scalpel down, she reached in and pulled back the two flaps of flesh that carried with them all the years of fat Malcom had stored over his lifetime. It was just as if she were opening two barn doors. The woosh of gas that escaped from the abdomen filled the room. It's putrid smell didn't faze the doctor. She had prepared for it. She had put a dab of menthol cream below her nostrils to mask the stench.

Reaching inside the cavity, Marianne systematically began to remove, one-by-one, each of the organs. Each organ was examined, then weighed. Her assistant John had begun the task of cutting small pieces from each of the organs to be sent to the lab for analyses. The heart, the kidneys, the bladder were all placed neatly on the tray for him. When the stomach was removed, he sliced it open and drained its' contents into a bag for the lab.

"Ah, this is what I've been looking for," Bevan said as she held the man's quivering liver in her hand. Bringing it up to her face, she took time to examine it very carefully. An analysis of the liver would hopefully confirm what she already expected.

She slipped on a set of lighted magnifying glasses. Slowly she scanned the surface of the skin. The neck, the arms, the groin. She instinctively knew it had to be somewhere. When she got to the thighs of the legs, she spotted it. At approximately the middle of the right thigh there was an ever-so small puncture wound. Finding the wound confirmed it. Malcom Blatchford died as a direct result of an illegal act. He had been injected with a substance that resulted in his death. By the look of the liver and with her years of experience, she was sure the offending syringe would have been filled with insulin. All it would take now would be to wait for the lab results to return.

"John," she directed. "Have the lab put a rush on those tissue samples. I need those results STAT!"

*****

When she returned to her office she called out to her assistant, "Marjorie, come in here for a moment, and bring your notepad."

She had no intention of waiting for the official lab results. "Check my calendar and schedule an official Coroner's Inquest into the death of a Malcom Blatchford. I want it set up as soon as possible."

"Alright," Marjorie replied as she wrote on her pad. "And who do you want there?"

Bevan thought for a moment. "This is pretty straightforward. We don't need to make a big production out of this." It was far better to keep the inquest small she thought to herself. She had her proof that a 'Death Angel' existed, there was no need to make things any more complicated than they had to be. "Issue summonses for both Dr. Coleus and Dr. Fletcher. Find out from Jason who the hospital nurse on duty was the night Blatchford died and include her."

"Is that all?" Marjorie asked.

"Let me see," she thought for a moment. "Make sure Jason is there, of course." Then as an afterthought, "Also you better issue an invitation to the police

Sergeant Reindle. She'll have a definite interest in the outcome," Bevan added.

*****

The room was cold and bare of any trappings except for a lone flag that rested in it's stand against the wall. Dr. Bevan looked at the small group of people huddled in the few available wooden chairs in front of her. A quick scan told her they were all here. Drs. Coleus and Fletcher sat together on the right side. Behind them sat a woman who Marianne assumed was the night Duty Nurse from the hospital.

On the left side Dr. Bevan was annoyed to see her senior investigator, Jason Adler, sitting way too close to Sergeant Reindle. She watched for a moment as the Sergeant laughingly leaned over to whisper something in Jason's ear. What ever was said caused a large grin to take shape across Jason's face and a noticeable scowl to form across Marianne's.

"Is anyone here from the Blatchford family?" Bevan asked the recording clerk who was positioned beside her.

The clerk pointed. "The woman in the back is his wife," she answered.

"Alright, let's begin," Bevan directed.

The clerk rose to address the group. "This inquest into the death of Malcolm Blatchford is now in session.

Regional Medical Examiner Dr. Marianne Bevan presiding."

Jason saw that his boss was waiting patiently for Claire and him to settle down. He smiled at Dr. Bevan as he gave Claire a slight nudge with his elbow. Claire straightened up. When she looked to Marianne she silently mouthed 'Sorry'.

Dr. Bevan began her opening remarks. "The purpose of this inquiry is to determine the reason for the untimely death of Mr. Blatchford. While this inquiry is purposely held in an informal setting, it is expected that all involved will act in a manner befitting the solemness this case deserves. I have not asked for a police presence, because I do not feel it is necessary. But be warned," she stated. "I do have it in my power to meter out swift justice if required." She waited a few moments to let her warning sink in.

"I would like to ask Janice Blatchford to come forward," Bevan directed.

The woman in the back row slowly rose and moved forward to the front of the room.

"Mrs. Blatchford. First, I want to extend to you my most heart felt condolences on your loss," Marianne offered.

The clerk stood and produced an aged bible, "Will you please place your right hand on the bible and repeat after me." The required oath was stated and affirmed by the widow.

"Mrs. Blatchford, do you need a chair?" Bevan asked.

"No, thank you I'm alright," came the response.

Marianne led the widow through a series of questions to determine the medical condition of the woman's husband before he was admitted to the hospital. When completed, Mrs. Blatchford was thanked and returned to her seat.

"I would now ask Dr. Mark Coleus to come forward," Marianne stated.

After Dr. Coleus had been sworn in, "I wish to inform you Doctor, that the complete hospital file of Mr. Blatchford has already been officially entered into the record." Dr. Bevan wanted to make sure that Coleus got the message that he was being watched.

*****

Nurse Michele Rice was surprised to hear that there was going to be an official inquest into the death of Mr. Blatchford. Dr. Fletcher had let it slip, when he was doing his rounds, that he had been subpoenaed to attend. Why only Blatchford, she thought to herself. There hadn't been any fuss over any of the other deaths. She was thankful that so far, she wasn't caught up in the investigation, but an official inquest was far too big for her to ignore. She wanted to know what was going on.

“And what time did you say this inquest was?” she casually asked.

“It’s scheduled for first thing in the morning. It’s going to be a hassle to get there on time,” Dr. Fletcher grumbled. “I’m going to have to leave here, rush home, change and get cleaned up. Then on top of that, there’s the morning rush hour traffic I’m going to have to fight to get to the other side of town. All without getting any sleep,” he moaned.

In her head, Michele was calculating how much time she would have. No, there wouldn’t be enough time. If she wanted to hear first hand what was going on, she’d have to leave directly from the hospital as soon as her shift relief showed up.

*****

Michele tried unsuccessfully to slip in as quietly as she could. She had hoped not to draw any unwanted attention to herself. Her plan was to sneak in, find out why Blatchford’s death warranted an inquest when all the other’s had gone unnoticed, then sneak out with no one being any the wiser. She needed to know what made the authorities realize Blatchford had been murdered.

Out of the corner of her eye, Dr. Bevan caught movement from the back of the room. A middle-aged woman was trying to go unnoticed. The fact that the woman was still dressed in what obviously was full nurses garb had instantly tweaked her interest.

"Thank you, Nurse James, you can return to your seat," Bevan directed to the nurse that was on duty the night Blatchford was killed. Marrianne checked her short list of witnesses and she had heard from them all. The wife, Drs. Coleus and Fletcher, and the night nurse Joanna James, there was no one else scheduled to give evidence. '*Who was this woman? Why was she here? Whatever it was'*, Bevan thought to herself, '*must have been important enough that the woman didn't take the time required to go home and get changed'*.

Michele could see that she was being watched. She slouched down as low as she could in her chair.

Bevan glanced over to her investigator hoping to get some sign of clarification as to who this woman was, but that was useless. Jason was sitting there with a stupid grin on his face, not paying any attention to what was going on.

"Young lady. Yes, you at the back. Can you please stand?" Bevan directed. Everyone in the room turned to see who it was that the Doctor had called out.

"That's Nurse Rice," Dr. Fletcher volunteered. "She was the other nurse on duty that night on the ward."

When Bevan heard this, she immediately looked to Adler. The look in her eyes carried the distinct message that he had screwed up again by only issuing summonses to the one nurse on duty when it should have been to both. She'd have more to say about this later.

"Is this true?" Bevan asked.

'Damn it. This was a mistake. I shouldn't have come'. "Yes Mam," Michele answered.

"Please come forward, and be sworn in," Bevan ordered.

Once Michele was sworn in, "For the record, please state your name," the clerk said.

"My name is Michele Rice."

Dr. Bevan could see anxiety was written all over the woman's face. She could tell the woman was afraid of something. What was it? "Are you a nurse at St. Luke's Hospital and were you working the night Mr. Blatchford died?"

"Yes mam."

"This session was led to believe that Nurse Joanna James, was the nurse on duty that night," Marianne wanted clarification as to how this woman was involved.

“Nurse James and I were partners both working on the ward that night.” Michele had started out wanting to be very careful as to what she said and not offer up anything extra then what was asked. That was until she got an idea. This might just work out alright, she thought.

“Can you give us your recollection of exactly what you remember involving Mr. Blatchford that night?”

“Well,” Michele started. “It was a busy night and Joanna and I were being run off our feet.” She continued to spell out the details of the night. “ … and Mr. Blatchford was constantly ringing his bell. The number of times we checked on him there was nothing wrong and he just wanted someone to talk with. And we simply didn’t have time to idly sit with him. There was just too much to do.”

“Please continue,” Dr. Bevan prompted.

“We have an orderly who often works on our floor.” Michele didn’t want to appear to be too eager to give up information. She wanted to force Dr. Bevan to lead her into saying what she wanted to say.

“Yes, go on,” Dr. Bevan encouraged. “What about this orderly?”

When Detective Reindle heard the word ‘orderly’ mentioned she perked up. She leaned forward in her chair to catch everything that was said concerning an orderly. She gave a slight wave towards Bevan to catch her attention. When the Doctor glanced her way, she silently mouthed the word 'Name?"

"And what is the name of this orderly?" Bevan asked. She was annoyed that Claire was telling her what to do, but she realized they all needed to know the name of this orderly.

"Andrew Brompton," Michele answered, acting as if the name had been dragged out of her.

'*Yes*,' Claire thought. '*I've got you now*!'

"So, what's important about this orderly? Why do you mention him?" Bevan wanted to know the full story.

"Andrew is kind of special" Michele continued. "He likes to sit with patients and talk with them."

"And how long after this 'Andrew' sat and talked to Mr. Brompton, did you notice something was wrong?"

"I'm not sure when Andrew left Mr. Brompton's room, but the next time we did our rounds, we found he had passed away."

"Thank you, Ms. Rice. This has been very informative," Dr. Bevan said. "You may go back to your chair."

Dr. Bevan took a couple of moments to gather up her papers and compose herself. "It is the finding of this inquest that Mr. Malcolm Blatchford died by a lethal injection of insulin administered illegally by person or person's unknown. The finding of this inquest will be turned over to the proper legal authority for further investigation."

Sergeant Reindle could barely contain herself. At last, she now had the proof she had been looking for to arrest Andrew Brompton.

Chapter 17

Detectives Swan and Morrison fought with the paperwork at their desks as they waited for their Sergeant to return. She had left word that she would be attending a Coroner's Inquest for most of the morning but would be in as soon as it was finished.

It was well into the afternoon before Claire finally arrived at her office. When the doors of the elevator opened, she took a moment before exiting. The glow on her face showed she was still caught up in the events of the morning. So far it had turned out to be a near perfect day for her.

At first, she thought having to go to the inquest was going to be a dull, boring waste of her time. She had expected Dr. Bevan would be pumped up with her own sense of importance while she'd be forced to sit quietly and watch as Bevan performed for all in attendance, especially for Jason. Instead, what happened had surprised her. Other than the odd sideways glance from the doctor, Bevan had stayed laser focused on the task at hand. After all the mundane testimonies were given, not only did the doctor make the declaration that a murder had been committed, but Bevan had also laid the killer squarely in her lap.

And Jason, well, just the thought of him made her blush. Instead of returning to his office at the end of the session, he had invited her to a celebratory lunch. The normal practice after an inquest would have had him huddled together with Dr. Bevan rehashing the results and planning for their next moves. But not this time. He had taken Claire to a small Greek Restaurant that had intimate dark booths behind thick curtains that kept the light from the sun and prying eyes out. They had spent a long, wonderfully romantic lunch together, crowded into a tiny booth. When she thought back on it, it was all so childish. They had really talked about nothing; only silly words were passed back and forth between the two of them. They didn't have dessert. Jason had promised her they would have dessert later, and the crushing kiss he had given her told her it would be deliciously sinful.

"Morning boys," Claire stated when she passed by the detectives' desks.

It had been a long time since the two had seen their Sergeant this happy.

"It's not morning anymore," Tony replied, but Claire paid no notice to the jab. She was in too good a mood to have anyone ruin this day for her.

"I don't envy you when you tell her about what you did with Brompton. When she comes down from the high she's on, it's going to be quite a crash," Swan mocked his partner.

"Hold on," Morrison snapped back. "As I recall, there were two of us in that interview room."

"As a matter of fact, I do recall. And letting him go was your decision, ol-buddy."

"Thanks a lot!" Tony took a deep breath. "Alright, we might as well get this over with," he said as he picked up his notepad and headed towards the Sergeant's office.

Swan followed, a good two steps behind his partner, grinning the whole way.

*****

Sergeant Reindle didn't notice the pensive look on Tony's face, but she did notice the grin that was spread across Julian's. Did she appear to be so happy that he was mocking her? She tried to spin her chair around to give herself time to pull herself together, but when she returned to face him, she thought it didn't work. His grin was still there.

"What are you grinning about?" she directed towards Swan. She had attempted to put a sternness in her voice, but she just couldn't fake it today. She was just too damn happy.

"Oh nothing," he replied. "I think my partner here has something he wants to tell you."

Claire looked over towards Tony. The shine in her eyes only added to the tension he was feeling.

"I'm waiting," she said.

Tony bit his lip, this wasn't going to be easy. He started, "It's about Andrew Brompton ..."

Claire interrupted her detective before he could get his message out. "Good, that's exactly who I was going to talk to you two about." She went on to relay the events of the inquest, " ... and Bevan declared Blatchford's death a definite homicide ... and Brompton was the last one in the room before Blatchford was discovered dead. I want you two to go downstairs to the holding cells and formally charge Brompton with 'First Degree Murder'."

Detective Swan had been doing the best he could to hold himself together, but he just couldn't help it. "That might be a little hard to do, don't you think?" he chuckled at his partner.

The Sergeant looked to Morrison, then to Swan, then back to Morrison. The shine that was in her eyes was now gone. "What have you done?"

"I was trying to tell you," Tony replied. "We had to let Brompton go."

Claire's eyes sprung wide open with disbelief. "You're kidding me. We've just been handed a serial killer on a silver platter and now you're telling me you had to let him go?"

"It's not that simple," Tony tried to defend himself. "Let me explain," he pleaded.

Claire sat back in her chair and crossed her arms over her chest. "This better be good. It better be damn good," she threatened.

Tony paused for a moment, took a deep breath to steady himself and began his tale. "We had Brompton in for questioning with the full intent to hold him for 72 hours as our prime suspect ..."

"Then why the hell didn't you?" Claire yelled. "That's what you were supposed to do!"

"I'm getting to it, if you'll let me finish without interrupting," Tony stated, his voice filled with frustration. "As we were interviewing the man, it became clear that Brompton wasn't quite what you'd call normal."

"Of course he's not normal. He's a serial killer!" Claire blurted out.

"That's not what I meant," Tony continued. "Andrew is what I think they call 'Feeble Minded'. We could easily see he had no grasp of what we were asking or of the seriousness of his answers. He agreed to everything

Julian put to him. He thought we were questioning him because he was in bed with some nurse."

"Let me get this straight," Claire stated. "Because he agreed that he was a killer, you took it upon yourself to just up and let him walk free?"

Tony's frustration with his Sergeant had now turned to a slow, burning rage. He did what he thought was the right thing to do. She wasn't there so he knew she didn't understand. But still, wherever she had spent her afternoon, it didn't give her the right to belittle him this way.

"Look," he stated. "Either you trust me or you don't. It really doesn't matter. I know I did the right thing by letting him go, and that's the end of it," he challenged.

Claire thought for a long moment. Getting angry and arguing with her detectives wasn't accomplishing a thing. If she was ever going to bring an end to this case so she could get on with her life with Jason, she would have to put her personal feeling aside and start thinking with her head and not her heart. If what Tony had said was true, then he did do the right thing, she realized. "Alright," she said. "What do you want to do now? We can't just let a suspected serial killer walk around free without doing anything."

"I think we need to get him tested by a professional," Tony answered.

"Have a couple of uniforms bring him in," she directed as she picked up her phone. "I'll see if I can get the DA to issue an 'Emergency Court Order' to have him checked over by one of our shrinks."

*****

"Where were you?" Dr. Bevan, clearly upset, asked her Investigator. "I was expecting to go over the results of this morning's findings with you?"

Jason looked up from his desk to see his boss standing in the doorway to his office. He had sat down only moments before. He was still a little flushed from the mad dash he had just finished as he tried to get back to his office before Bevan noticed he wasn't there. When he and Claire had finally parted at the Greek Restaurant, he hadn't realized it was so late in the afternoon. It was so easy to lose track of time whenever he was with her.

"I had a couple of personal things I had to take care of," he answered in an off the cuff manner with the hope that Bevan would let it go and not pry any deeper.

Dr. Bevan wasn't fooled. From the display she watched during the inquest she had a pretty good idea why Jason was nowhere to be found for most of the afternoon. She had watched Sergeant Reindle put on a sickening exhibition of herself as she clung to Jason for most of this morning's proceedings.

Jason could feel the tension build as he waited.

"You look a little flushed and out of breath," she toyed with him. "Are you alright? You have to be careful. You know there's a lot of things you could pick up if you're not careful." The dig Marianne shot wasn't subtle at all.

"I'm fine. What is it you want?" Jason had picked up on the jab Bevan had thrown, but he wasn't about to give her the satisfaction of acknowledging it.

Marianne turned to leave, "Come into my office. We have some work we need to be doing. That is if you feel up to it."

Jason didn't like the abuse his boss had started giving him lately. For now, he knew it was best if he kept his head down and continued to move forward. The pay was good. In fact, the pay was extremely good. And, on top of that, the work was challenging and kept his interest high everyday. But, if Dr. Bevan didn't change her ways soon, he would have a decision to make. Once this 'Angel' business was over, and he and Claire were together, he wouldn't be putting up with Bevan's antics for very long.

*****

Dr. Bevan picked up one of the papers off her desk and handed it to Adler.

Jason looked at it and was confused. To him it looked like a pile of scribbling. “What’s this?”

“While you weren’t here, I spent the time jotting down some random ideas of where we go next,” she answered. “I’m interested in your opinion.”

Jason studied the paper again. He could make out the odd word, but he couldn’t make sense of what he was looking at. “You’re going to have to decipher this for me. You doctors must take scribbling lessons when you go through medical school. I don’t think anyone would be able to read this.”

Bevan took the paper back. “We need a plan if we are going to put an end to the needless deaths that are happening over at St. Luke’s. We can’t go shooting off in all directions and hope that we’ll stumble upon something.”

“I agree. What is it you’re thinking of doing?”

“Well,” Marianne started to read off her scribblings. “From what we have learned at this morning’s inquest, there’s a couple of key people that we know so far are involved.”

“I don’t know,” Jason hesitated. “There’s a lot more people floating around inside that hospital. I think it might be a mistake if we limit ourselves to only the few people we know about.”

Marianne thought for a moment, “You might be right. We didn’t know anything about that orderly, Andrew Brompton, until this morning.”

“That’s who the police are zeroing in on,” Jason piped in. “When he came up in testimony this morning, Sergeant Reindle nearly jumped out of her seat.”

“I saw that,” Bevan mumbled.

“Shouldn’t we let that play out before we do anything?” Jason asked. “We don’t want to be accused with interfering with a police investigation.”

“Hmm, that’s one approach,” Marianne said. Then thinking to herself, ‘*And we certainly wouldn’t want to do anything that would interfere with your little friend, would we’*. “But my gut is telling me we shouldn’t sit by idly as we wait for someone else to do their work. Did you notice that nurse,” she checked her paper, “Michele Rice?”

“I saw her. What about her?”

“She interests me. She was still wearing her work uniform indicating she came directly from work. Why would she do that? She was there for a purpose.” Bevan closed her eyes and travelled back in her memory to the inquest. “And another thing that was strange. When I was questioning her, I felt she was trying to manipulate me. She wanted me to ask her questions that would allow her to bring that orderly into the picture. Why would she do that? No one else mentioned anything about an orderly."

"Maybe she was the only one that knew about him," Jason answered.

Marianne shook her head. "No, I don't buy that. Hospitals are notoriously close-knit communities. No one sneezes without everyone else knowing about it. She brought Brompton up for a reason."

"Well, if she did what was the reason?"

"That's what I want you to find out. Start by meeting with the head of the Nursing Dept. See if you can find out the background of Rice. Where did she come from? How long has she been working at St. Luke's. Is there anything in her record that we should know about?"

"And what are you going to be doing while I'm looking into Rice?"

"I think I'm going to go back to basics. I'm going to get a dump of the information from the hospital records for all the sudden deaths that have happened in the last month. Maybe I can find some similarities that will lead to what the motive for the killings were."

Chapter 18

Jason Adler stepped up to the reception desk, "I'd like to see the Head of the Nursing Department please," he said as he flashed his credentials in front of the receptionist.

"That would be Ms. Hopkins. Is she expecting you?" the girl asked. "I don't see an appointment listed on her calendar," she declared as she scanned her computer.

"I don't have an appointment, but if you tell her I'm here, I'm sure she will want to see me." Being from the County Medical Examiner's Office carried a lot of weight whenever he visited any of the area hospitals. His boss, Dr. Bevan, was well known as someone you didn't want to fool with.

"Ms. Hopkins, there's a gentleman from the County Medical Examiner's Office here who says he needs to speak with you," the girl said over the phone. "Yes, of course. I'll send him right in."

When Jason entered the office, Doris practically leaped over her desk to welcome him. "Good morning," she greeted with her hand extended. "I'm Doris Hopkins and I'm the Head of the Nursing Department here at St. Luke's."

Jason shook the woman's large, manly hand. "My name is Jason Adler and I work for Dr. Marianne Bevan, the County Medical Examiner."

"And how is Dr. Bevan?" Doris pretended to show an interest. "I've had the pleasure to attend a number of her lectures. She's quite a remarkable woman."

"That she is," Jason replied.

"Here, where's my manners. Please have a seat and make yourself comfortable. Can I get you a coffee or anything?" Doris had no idea what Dr. Bevan's office could want to talk with her about, but whatever it was, she wanted to be seen as being fully cooperative. She had heard tales of people who had ended up on the wrong side of the Doctor.

Jason grinned to himself. He was used to people bending over backwards when they heard that Bevan was involved. "No, nothing for me, thank you."

Doris resumed her position behind her desk. "Well, what can I possibly do for you?"

Now that the pleasantries were over, Jason thought to himself, we'll see how cooperative this woman was going to be. "Dr. Bevan has asked me to inquire about one of your nurses, a Michele Rice."

Doris's mind began to race. What would Bevan want with Michele? She had checked her resume and although dated, it was accurate. Michele had caused no problems, was punctual and had worked well alongside all of the doctors. "This is highly unusual. Why would the Medical Examiner want to know about Nurse Rice? Our employee files are confidential and I'm not sure I'm allowed to discuss an individual's record."

This was going to take a little bit of work, Jason realized. With a touch a sweet talk and a hint of threats, he was sure he'd have Doris singing her head off. "I understand your files are confidential and Dr. Bevan wouldn't be asking unless she felt it was important. She was hoping that we could do this quietly and not have to get a lot of people involved. And I can assure you that anything you tell me is only for Dr. Bevan's ears." Jason faked starting to get up from his chair, "but if you like, the Doctor will have no problem issuing a formal 'Order to Comply'."

Hopkins had no desire to have anyone from the hospital administration or legal group involved sticking their noses into her department. She had been around long enough to realize that whenever you turn over a rock, you never know what might pop out and bite you. "Hold on," she piped up. "If the information is only for the good Doctor, I see no reason we can't work something out." If Bevan was prepared to issue a formal request, this must be serious. Doris could think of only one thing that would have the Medical Examiner demanding that kind of information. Warning bells started to sound in her brain. It would be far better, she thought, if she were the one to give out the information, then she would also be the one who had control over what Bevan would be told. She would need to be very careful with what she said. "Does this have anything to do with the recent number of unexpected deaths that have been occurring?" she asked casually, not wanting to appear as if she was overly concerned with it.

The attempted casual remark didn't fool Jason. He picked up that this woman was very interested in what was going on with the rise in hospital deaths. Dr. Bevan might be interested in Nurse Rice, but he was now suddenly interested in Doris Hopkins.

*****

In her office, Sergeant Reindle mulled over the report she had received concerning Andrew Brompton. If the size of the report was any indication, the Group that was under contract with the Regional Assistant DA's office had really earned their money with Andrew. It was a thick, multi-paged package, crammed full with a lot of medical jargon she really didn't understand. In trying to read the report, Claire had picked up that Andrew had been 'Observed' by a team that consisted of a Psychiatric Doctor, Dr. Harry Manter, and two

Mental Therapists. The team must be good at what they do, Claire thought, as she noticed the alphabet of letters that were tacked onto the end of Dr. Manter's name. She wasn't sure what she had expected when she had pushed the Assistant DA to have Andrew checked over, but it certainly wasn't this. What she really was looking for, was a clear-cut medical evaluation that stated Andrew was 'Competent' so that he could be charged and stand trial for committing multiple murders. Either that or he was a 'nut case' that needed to be secured in a mental facility. Either way, Andrew would be locked away and the deaths at St. Luke's would be stopped. She'd be able to close the 'Angel' case and finally get on to live the life she dreamed of living. No matter how many times she read over the report, all she saw was '*Medical Gobbly Gook'*. She couldn't see the answer she so badly wanted to find.

"Jason," she said over the phone, "are you doing anything special this evening?"

The phone call surprised Jason, and without knowing why Claire was asking him, he didn't want to commit himself. "Why, what have you in mind?"

"Unfortunately work," she stated. She went on to explain the report and how she needed someone with his expertise to help her decipher what it was trying to say.

"Why don't you just bring it over here to my office? I can look it over and let you know what I think," he offered.

Claire hesitated. "No, I really don't feel like getting tangled up with your boss today. This report already has me on edge. I don't need Bevan's head games to tip me over."

After a long pause where she waited for Jason to say something, but when he didn't, she came up with a solution on her own. "How about this? You come over to my apartment tonight after work and I'll cook you a homemade dinner. I am a pretty good cook," she added, trying to tempt him. "Then we can relax and go over the report together."

Jason had to admit it was a pretty good offer since he rarely cooked for himself. "Sounds tempting," he said. "And I believe I promised you dessert, didn't I?"

"You help me find the answer I need in this report and you'll have more dessert than you can handle."

When she left work at the end of the day, she had the 'Brompton' report tucked securely under her arm. "I may be a little late in the morning," she mentioned to her detectives as she hurried towards the elevator. She had a lot to do before Jason came over.

*****

Although her apartment was spacious with plenty of room to move around in, unfortunately, her 'Galley' style kitchen was not. The narrow kitchen had barely enough room for one person to try to pull the 'Homestyle' meal together that she had promised Jason. And when she had told him that she was a pretty good cook, she had really stretched the truth. Claire remembered what her mother had told her many years ago … *'When in doubt, make something light and colorful rather than heavy and overly fancy … but always make sure you include really good wine!'*

Tonight, she planned to go with a light salad, with fresh greens and red baby tomatoes that would be covered with a splash of tangy vinaigrette dressing as an appetizer. Paired with this she had picked up a refreshing dry white wine that the merchant assured her would open the taste buds of her man. For the main course she worked on preparing grilled chicken breast, a side of roasted peppers along with a few stocks of asparagus with just a trimming of hollandaise sauce. With this there was the bottle of 'Sauvignon Blanc Wine' that was chilling in her refrigerator. As for dessert, she snickered to herself, that was up to Jason and the little surprise she had purchased some time ago. She eagerly looked forward to seeing the effect her matching set of spicy, flame red lingerie, which left very little to the imagination, would have on Jason, when he slowly undressed her later tonight.

The knock on her door told her he was here.

*****

Dr. Bevan was spending her evening alone in her office. Earlier she had her assistant, Marjorie, run down to the local deli and pick up a 'Bagel with cream cheese and lox along with a crème soda' for her to munch on. It wasn't much and certainly wasn't gourmet, but it was all she needed. She rarely cooked and existed mainly on a diet of restaurant take out meals.

In front of her there was a stack of computer print outs that she had received from St. Luke's Hospital. The stack contained the records of all the deaths that had occurred at the hospital over the last month. Her task for this evening was to separate the papers into two separate piles. One, with all the deaths that she determined were normal, and expected from patients who had reached their end of life. The second would be the deaths that were deemed to be sudden, unexpected and really shouldn't have happened.

Unfortunately, from the amount of paper in front of her, it looked like it was going to be a long evening. Taking a sip of her crème soda through a straw, she wondered where her Investigator was this evening. Reading through all these files would go so much faster if he were here.

*****

It had been a long evening for Marianne. When she looked at the two stacks of files now before her, she let out a heavy sigh filled with satisfaction. She felt all the effort she had put in had been worth it. For the first time since she had acknowledged the possibility of an active 'Death Angel' operating in St. Luke's Hospital, she had what she considered a true list of the victims. And, with no surprise to her, the list was considerably more than what Dr. Coleus had indicated in the weekly mortality reports he had issued.

She was now ready for the real work to begin. Every page of every file in the 'Angel' pile would have to be read, then read again and possibly again. Somewhere in the stack of paper lay the reason for the unwanted deaths and she had to find it. She knew the first step in her hunt was to find the 'Why'. Only when she had uncovered the 'Why' could she move on to discovering the all-important 'Who'.

*****

As soon as she opened her apartment door Jason blurted out, "Where's this report you want me to look over for you?" He was direct to the point, all business.

Claire was stunned. She had expected a warm greeting ... 'Hello Baby' ... along with a deep lip crushing kiss and a playful tap on her backside. It would have been nice to hear him say ... 'Hmm, smells good. I'm starving' ... as if he were coming home to her after a tough day at the office.

"Come in. The report's on the living room coffee table. I made us a nice dinner with some wine that I thought we could enjoy together first."

"Later," Jason shrugged the offer off. On his way over to the apartment he had been thinking about Andrew. The more he had thought about the orderly, the more his appetite had slipped away from him. "I'm interested in this report of the orderly. It could give us a valuable key to know what's going on at that hospital."

Claire slumped down in one of her side chairs. She watched as Jason eagerly dug into the report.

He mumbled to himself as he read "... aha ... aha ... yes ... interesting ..." When he was done, he held the report up towards Claire, "What makes you think this screwed up boy is the Bittman killer, let alone the Death Angel?"

Claire was surprised with the question. "Of course, he's the killer. He's been our number one suspect right from the beginning. The only question is does the report say he's competent to stand trial or do we move to lock him up right away?"

Jason shook his head. "If I believe this report, there's no way Andrew Brompton could have killed anyone."

"It has to be him. He has motive. Coleus killed his father. He has opportunity. In his job as orderly in the hospital he has free access to go anywhere without anyone taking any notice of him. And besides, for God's sake, he likes to sit and talk to dying people."

Jason sat and looked at Claire.

She was puzzled with the look on Jason's face. She couldn't make out whether he was angry with her or what his problem was. "What's the matter?"

The look Jason was giving Claire was the look of disappointment. He had thought she was smarter than this. "Have you really given this a lot of thought?"

"God damn it! Of course, I've given this a lot of thought. It's all I've been thinking about for days."

"There's no point in getting angry with me. I'm telling you from everything I see in this report there is no way Andrew killed anyone."

Claire was furious. She reached out and grabbed the report from Jason's hand. "If you're so smart, what does this report say?"

Jason paid no attention to Claire's fit of anger. He calmly, in an even voice, started to rhyme off the report's details. " ... Andrew bares no resentment towards Dr. Coleus. To him he lost two fathers because they were sick. His only concern is that while both his fathers were ill, caring for them took a heavy tole on his mother. He's glad the men died, it resulted in him not having to share his mother. He had her all to himself. As for talking to dying people, what he was doing was telling them it was ok to die. He wasn't killing them. The report goes on to state that when they tested Andrew's IQ, he fell into the 'Low Intelligence' category. All the deaths in the hospital have been extremely clever. Think about it. Knowing that an insulin overdose can kill, hacking the hospital computer system to insert false doctor orders, triggering heart attacks. All these things are way above Andrew's capabilities. You're not looking for a 'Dim-Wit'. You're looking for a highly skilled, clever person who has some hidden grudge that is driving them to commit murder."

Claire's mind was racing. Everything was wrong. A wave of doubt washed over her. How could she have been so stupid. What was wrong with her. She broke the number one rule of investigating ... '*Follow the facts*' ... She had let her personal life drive her to make bad decisions.

"Well, are we going to eat? I'm starving."

The dinner would be cold, Claire thought. And it looked like her lingerie would also be wasted.

*****

"Dr. Bevan," Jason paused at her office doorway. "Can I talk to you for a minute? I have some information that I think you should know."

The sudden sound of a voice startled her. She had thought she was alone. The only sounds she had been hearing had been the rattling of the building ventilation system as the fans cycled on and off continuously throughout the night.

“What in the world are you doing here at this time of night?” the doctor asked. “Haven’t you anything better to be doing with your evenings?”

Jason did have something better that he should have been doing, but in his eagerness to redeem himself in the Doctor’s eyes, he had turned it down. Inherently he knew he had made the wrong decision, but it was a decision he had to make. He knew it saddened his love, Claire. He had seen it in her face. Her eyes had almost filled with tears when he left her apartment. If they were ever going to pull together the love life they both wanted, the ‘Angel’ had to be stopped. He hated to admit it, but he knew Dr. Bevan was right. With his love and desire for Claire pulling at him, he hadn’t been focusing all his abilities into his job. He hoped Claire would understand and wait.

*****

Jason went on to tell his boss of the results of the ‘Competency Report’ that had been completed on Andrew Brompton.

Dr. Bevan sat quietly and listened. On occasion she would nod her head in agreement with what Jason was telling her. "And who did you say completed the evaluation?" she asked.

"A team headed up by a Dr. Harry Manter. I've never heard of him, but the report he generated appeared to be very through."

"Hmm. Although I can't say I know him personally, I have met him on occasion at a number of conferences. I believe he carries enough validity that if he rules out Andrew, we can believe him."

As she sat behind her desk, Marianne absent mindedly began to wring her hands together. Back and forth, back and forth. "It keeps gnawing at me," she began. "I can't stop wondering why that Nurse Rice would even bring up anything about Andrew Brompton during her testimony. She had to have known that he wasn't a smart man as Dr. Manter stated in his report. I know she did it on purpose. But why?" More hand wringing and now she started to bite on her lip. Something wasn't right and Marianne didn't like it.

"What have you found out about Rice?" she asked.

"I met with a Doris Hopkins, who is the Director of Nursing at the hospital. All I was able to get out of her was that Nurse Rice has all the proper credentials and is liked by those she works with. I sensed that there is some type of relationship between Doris and Michele. She seemed to be overly protective and guarded in what she said about Rice," Jason reported. "But, between you and me," Jason added, "I picked up strange vibes from this Hopkins woman. There's more to her than she was letting on."

The last statement Jason had made interested Marianne. "In what way?"

"I don't know. It's just a feeling I picked up on," he answered. "Starting tomorrow I have to spend a lot more time around that hospital."

"Good. And I've got a lot more work to do with these files." Bevan rose from her desk, "But I think we should both go home, get a good night's sleep, so we can start fresh in the morning."

Jason didn't know how much sleep he would get. He was pretty sure thoughts of Claire would haunt him throughout the night.

*****

"I thought you were going to be late?" Detective Swan commented.

Claire looked at her watch and saw that she wasn't late. She was in fact considerably earlier than her normal time.

"I couldn't sleep and decided I might as well come in."

It was true that she couldn't sleep, but not for the reason she had thought would have happened. Her eyes were still red and puffy from the long night she spent in bed, alone. There had been no love making or even any of the romantic cuddling that she had hoped for.

Last night, as soon as Jason had wolfed down the dinner and just half a glass of the wine she had served, he surprised her by leaving. The only show of affection he had shared with her was a quick peck on her cheek, then he was gone. He was more interested in rushing back to his office to tell his boss, Dr. Bevan, what he had discovered about Andrew Brompton than spending the night wrapped in her arms.

Lying in bed, still wearing her hot red lingerie, she had cried. Deep, gut-wrenching tears had wet her pillow. The romantic night that she had hoped for had proven to be one of the worse nights of her life. She was angry with that witch, Bevan, for pulling Jason away from her. She was angry with Jason for abruptly leaving, choosing to be with Bevan rather than with her. But, more than anything, she was angry with herself. She wanted so desperately to have a full, loving relationship with Jason that she had been willing to let him walk all over her.

"As soon as Morrison arrives, come into my office. We have a lot to talk about."

*****

Claire hesitated for a moment. "Tony," she wanted to be personable. "I'm afraid I owe you an apology. You were right about Andrew Brompton. The medical review we had subjected him to showed him to be incapable of being the hospital 'Angel'."

Detective Morrison smiled. He was pleased to be vindicated with the apology given to him by his Sergeant.

"But with the orderly now out of the picture, it leaves us without a prime suspect. Have either of you two got any ideas?" Claire asked.

"What about Coleus?" Detective Swan offered. "Ever since our first interview with him I've had the feeling he's hiding something."

"He definitely didn't want to turn over the 'Bittman' file when we asked him," Detective Morrison added. "And by what we learned about him when we interviewed that Nurse Lucy, he does have a history."

"Hmm," Claire thought. "Could be a possibility. Were you able to pick up anything from his financial records?"

"When our 'Forensic Accountants' went over his records, they did pick up a couple of things," Tony answered.

"Like what?" Claire asked impatiently. She was tired and didn't want to drag things out.

"Well, for the last couple of months there have been a number of large deposits made into his bank account. And the other thing they picked up on, was that as fast as the money was deposited, Coleus would withdraw it."

"Where do they think the money had been coming from?" Claire asked. "Getting money in your bank account isn't a crime unless we can prove where it came from," she cautioned.

"Julian and I turned the matter over to the 'Organized Crime' boys for them to chase. We should get an answer soon," Tony piped in.

Claire struggled to think with her brain slowly shutting down from lack of sleep. She tried to determine what the best course of action would be. "Alright," she stated once she had made up her mind. "With Coleus and the money angle, we'll leave him to the OC group to chase. They're better suited for that kind of investigation."

Detective Swan felt uneasy with his Sergeant's decision. "We're not going to just let Dr. Coleus go, are we?" he asked. "We know he's hiding stuff. Why don't we go after him?"

Claire took a hard look at her detective. She was amazed that he would ask such a question. This was not the morning to argue with her. "Let's get it through our heads," she spoke directly at Swan. "We work in Homicide. Our job is to track down killers. It's not to chase money laundering, bribes or what ever the hell Coleus has got himself into. We have a very skilled killer operating right under our noses. We need to leave the things that don't concern us and focus all our attention into nailing this 'Angel'." She paused to give her detectives a chance to say something. Morrison nodded his head in agreement, but Swan sat and never moved a muscle. Claire stared right through him. "Clear!"

"I guess so," he finally gave in.

*****

It had been an especially long night for Dr. Bevan. One in which she didn't get much sleep. She had far too many thoughts running wild in her brain which left her tossing and turning under a mountain of blankets. And now, this morning, she was paying the price for her sleepless night.

Her eyes, that had already started out sore from her lack of restful sleep, were further aggravated from her reading the stack of 'Angel' files which she had spread out all over the top of her desk. She had read each one several times in her quest to find the 'Why'. With no mirror to check, she was sure by now her eyes would be all red and puffy. Dr. Bevan knew she should be wearing glasses, all her recent eye tests had told her that, but her vanity just wouldn't allow her to wear them. She remembered the last time she was in her Optometrist Office. She had tried on several pair, one after another. With each one she had checked how they looked on her, and the one phrase that kept coming to her mind was 'Granny' glasses. Her body was aging fast enough, she didn't feel she needed to openly advertise the fact. Holding one of the files in her hand caused a frown to form on her face. When she was younger, back more years than she wanted to admit to, her hands were thought to be slender. Her long fingers, topped with just the slightest hint of nail polish color presented an elegant look. Now, that had changed. The long, bare fingers were fragile. The hand that was once white betrayed her. Now it showed a gray-blue pallor from the mase of bulging dark blue veins that snaked across under the thin film of skin. She remembered how when she used to greet people, she could clasp hands with them and return just as strong a grip as they would give her. Now she dreaded shaking peoples hands for fear they would squeeze hers' too hard. Although she fought to slow the outwardly signs of aging, it was a losing battle.

So far, from her study of the 'Angel' files she had learned three things. Things that she felt were important to know if she was ever going to determine who the 'Death Angel' was. First it was easy to see that the 'Angel's' victims were only men. None of the files she had picked out from the hospital medical records were of women. The other important thing she noticed was that the men that were killed were all mature, well advanced in their age. There was no sign of any young men being in the collection. And the third, perhaps most telling point, was all the victims were from the fourth floor of the hospital.

Chapter 19

Michele exclaimed in surprise, "Doris, I didn't expect to see you in here at this time of night." Michele had heard from other nurses that Doris had started prowling the hospital halls at night. Michele had been absorbed inputting the details of the medicine she had just administered to her patient, Mr. Crowley, into the hospital computer system. Crowley had been causing a nuisance until the sleeping tablets she had given him finally took hold. She hadn't noticed when Doris silently appeared beside her.

Doris liked Michele. She felt they were kindred spirits in the man-less love life they both shared. She thought they could trust each other with their most personal secrets. "I haven't been sleeping all that well since my husband's passing," she confided to Michele. "So rather than sit at home alone with only my cat, I thought I might as well come in and do some 'spot' checkups and maybe help make things run smoother for the night staff.

Michele wanted to be careful with what she said. She realized having the Director of Nursing on your side was a big bonus. A bonus she never knew when she might have to take advantage of. "Does this mean you felt you needed to check up on me?" she playfully asked.

"No, no. Of course not. I wanted to tell you that I had the Medical Examiner's Investigator, Jason Alder, stop by my office asking questions about you."

A sharp jab of worry shot up Michele's back. She decided she had better play coy. "Well, he's certainly pushing his luck," she lied. "That's what happens when you go out on a date with a guy. Right away, they think they own you."

"He's certainly a handsome one," Doris commented.

Michele quickly thought back to the inquest. Having never met Alder, she figured he must have been the one sitting over to the side that had that woman fawning all over him. "Yes but being handsome doesn't give him the right to use his position to check up on me."

Being probed by the Medical Examiner, she felt, had to be fallout from her attending the Malcolm Blatchford inquest. Her mistake had brought unwanted attention onto herself. She had hoped that by bringing Andrew into the picture during her testimony that she had successfully diverted focus away from herself and over onto him. She would have to talk with Andrew, she thought. She was curious what impact, if any, she had caused to be thrown his way.

"What kind of questions did Jason ask about me?" she asked trying to appear as being only casually interested.

"You being on a date with him explains a lot," Doris said buying into Michele's lie. "He didn't seem to be interested in your work, as I would have expected. He kept asking general questions about your background."

"Are you sure that's all he was doing?" Michele, unlike Doris, wasn't fooled. From the little bit she had seen of the Medical Examiner, Dr. Bevan, she knew Bevan wouldn't have her investigator running around wasting his time. He had to be hunting for something.

"If I were you," Doris cautioned. "I'd watch out for this guy. Take it from me, men aren't always what they appear to be."

"Oh, don't worry. I'll be watching out for him from now on, that's for damn sure," Michele declared.

*****

"I'm going on my break now," Michele called out to her partner. "Mr. Crowley has finally settled down into a deep sleep, so you shouldn't have any more problems with him."

"Alright," her partner answered. "I'll restock the medicine cart while you're gone so it'll be ready for the morning meds."

As she rode down in the elevator, Michele couldn't stop thinking about Jason Alder. She wanted to know the real reason for what he was after. Why had he been asking questions about her? She was confident that Doris had bought into her lie of Jason being an obsessive boyfriend and was sure Doris would be careful about what she told him about her.

When she entered the hospital cafeteria, she noticed Andrew slumped over a table by himself along the back wall. This would be as good a time as any to find out if anything had come out of her attempt to throw suspicion Andrew's way she thought.

"Andrew," Michele greeted as she deliberately placed her hand on his shoulder.

He looked up at her and Michele noticed he didn't flash his customary smile towards her. He was wearing a solemn, blank face, a face that she hadn't seen on him before.

"What's wrong?"

Andrew said nothing. He only looked at her with eyes showing signs of being on the verge of erupting in tears.

"You and I are friends," she comforted. "You know you can tell me anything. Now what's got you down?"

He openly burst into tears and slowly shook his head. "It's the doctors," he sobbed. "They tell me I can't live alone in my mother's house anymore."

The sobs were so strong that Michele wasn't sure she heard what he had said. "Now Andrew," she said softly. "Slow down. Take a deep breath and tell me what you're crying about."

Andrew stopped and obediently took a couple of deep breaths as Nurse Rice had told him to do.

"There, that's better," she said as she handed him a tissue to wipe his eyes. "Now tell me everything right from the start."

Andrew began his tale. Once he started talking he couldn't stop. His pain flowed out to his friend. " ... and the police took me to a doctor who asked me questions ... and they made me do all kinds of tests ... and then they told me I shouldn't be living alone and they were going to have to get me help ... and they were going to move me somewhere ..." Tears began flowing again. Andrew hid his face in his arms on the table. The noise of his sobs caused others in the cafeteria to glance his way to see what the commotion was all about.

'*Oh God,*' Michele thought to herself. '*Look what I've done to him.*' Seeing this innocent boy so utterly destroyed and knowing she was the one responsible for making it happen filled her with a wave of guilt. She never meant for this to happen. She had thought that the police would see that Andrew was an innocent and leave both of them alone. Instead, she had opened a door and now things were spinning out of control. She was being probed by Alder. Andrew was being hassled by the police. She had to do something, but what? She needed time to think. Precious time that she knew she couldn't afford to waste.

"Andrew, I want you to go home. Don't worry, I'll tell them that you felt sick and needed to go home," Michele instructed. "When I'm done work in the morning I'll come over to your house and we can figure out what to do. Does that sound alright?"

"I guess," he said. "And you'll come to my house to help me?"

"Yes, I promise," Michele answered. By morning she knew she'd have to have a plan and the plan had better be good.

*****

In the early hours of the morning, the day shift nurses arrived. "Anything special happen last night?" Berna, who was Michele's relief, asked.

"No, everything's logged in my shift report. There was a little problem with Mr. Crowley earlier, but he settled down and has been sleeping soundly all night," Michele reported.

"Alright, go home and get some sleep yourself," Berna called out.

"I hope so. I need it," Michele replied thinking there would be no sleep until after she visited with Andrew. "I forgot to mention," she called back. "Doris was in prowling around again last night."

"She's been doing that a lot lately. Now go get some sleep."

After Michele had left, "I'm going to check on Mr. Crowley," Berna informed her nursing partner. "He's been sleeping an awfully long time. He should be awake by now. He's got to be washed and changed before the breakfast trays arrive."

When Berna entered Crowley's room, she knew at once something was wrong. No one slept that soundly. There was no snoring or any sign of Mr. Crowley's chest moving. The prime give away was his eyes were wide open, blankly staring off into nothingness. Berna checked for a pulse. None. She felt the limp hand. Cold. Before she left the room to report that Mr. Crowley died sometime during the night, she pulled the bed sheet covering up over his head.

*****

When Michele stepped off the bus, it was a short block and a half walk to reach the front of Andrew's house. From what she could see by standing in front of it, she could already tell that Andrew needed help. In a rather normal, well cared for suburban neighborhood, his house stood out like a sore thumb. It had a rundown, neglected look that screamed for attention. The paint was peeling, the grass hadn't been cut in what looked like years and the flower garden, that at one time must have been lovely, filled with glorious color, was totally overrun by dark brown weeds. The large front wrap around porch which would have been perfect for sitting out on warm evenings to talk to neighbors as they walked by, was filled with trash. Michele could guess that if any neighbors walked by the house now, they'd be turning their heads in disgust.

She walked gingerly up to the front door, careful where she stepped, and knocked. She knocked again harder this time and heard the sound as it echoed throughout the house. The door creaked open a crack to expose a set of worried eyes. As soon as the eyes recognized Nurse Rice as being the one knocking, the door flew open.

"You've come!" Andrew squealed with delight. His face lit up with a smile that ran ear to ear. "Come in, come in," he said in a loud sing-song voice. Michele had never seen him so happy. When she stepped across the threshold she stopped. A slow look around showed her that the inside of the house was in as bad if not worse state than the outside.

On her way here from the hospital, on the crowded morning bus, Michele fought to try to come up with some plan to correct for the problems she had caused Andrew. But now, after seeing the condition of the house he lived in, maybe the police doctors were right. Maybe Andrew shouldn't be alone and maybe for his own good he should be moved somewhere that he could be taken care of. Even though she hated to admit it, a part of her knew that was the right thing to do.

"I promised you I would come," Michele answered him. Although when she had entered the house she had no plan, one was now working itself out in her brain. A plan that if done right, would be good for Andrew and also be very good for her.

"Can I make you a cup of tea?" Andrew offered. "My mother always had tea when ladies would visit her."

Michele wouldn't have minded a soothing cup of tea, but the smell that drifted out of the kitchen, made her decide to pass on the offer. "No, it's alright. Is there somewhere we can sit and talk?" she asked.

Andrew opened a side door. "You can sit in the sunroom. It's where my mother liked to sit."

The room was a surprise. Although it was dusty from not being used in a very long time, the large windows gave it a bright, inviting feel. From the look of the room, Michele was pretty sure Andrew never sat or even entered this room on his own.

She moved across the room and settled onto a green stuffed love seat that was angled so it provided a clear, unobstructed view outside onto the large backyard. Andrew stood in the room doorway, unsure as to what he was supposed to do. He never entered this room, even when his mother was alive. She used to tell him that this room wasn't for children. It was a special place for her to meet and talk with her lady friends. Everything in the room was exactly as she had left it.

Michele noticed the hesitancy displayed by Andrew. "Come over here and sit by me so we can talk," she said to him as she patted the dust covered cushion beside her.

Andrew never moved. His mother had told him quite clearly to never come in this room and he always obeyed what his mother had told him.

"Come on," Michele coaxed. "I won't bite. We can't talk if you're going to just stand in the doorway." The dust swirled in the air as she patted the cushion.

Andrew slowly, very sheepishly, with his head bowed low, moved to the love seat and sat beside Nurse Rice.

"There, that wasn't so hard, was it?" she said.

Andrew smiled. He liked Nurse Rice. She treated him as a person, not as a boy, like all the other doctors and nurses at the hospital did. Sitting in this special room, so close beside her that he could feel her body touch his, gave him a weird feeling. One that he had never felt before, and he liked it.

"Andrew," Michele started in a soft voice. She wanted to be careful that she didn't frighten him. Before she could attempt to launch her plan, she needed to probe for some details. "This is a very big house you have to be living in all by yourself."

He nodded in agreement. "It's my mother's house."

Although the house was now in a state of disrepair she needed to know, "How do you pay for it?"

Andrew was quite proud of himself. He knew the answer to Nurse Rice's question. When his mother had passed away, a long time ago, her lawyer had explained everything to him. "My mother's lawyer told me that my mother had taken care of everything. She arranged that her lawyer would pay all my bills and that I didn't have to worry about anything."

"And does this lawyer ever come to visit you? Does he check up on you to see how you are coping?"

"No," he answered. "I guess he's too busy. I've only seen him the one time and he got angry with me because he had to explain things to me a couple of times till I understood what he had been saying."

So far so good, Michele thought to herself. "Does anyone ever come to visit you?"

With a touch of sadness in his voice, "No," he answered. Then with a cheerful tone, "You're my first guest."

"Andrew," Michele said, feeling it was time to move forward with her plan. "Do you like living here all by yourself?"

"I miss my mother," he sighed. "When my mother was here with me everything was so different. Now there's just me."

"Do you think your mother would be happy if she came home and saw how you have kept her house? Remember when you told me that the police doctors told you that you couldn't live alone here by yourself?"

"They were very mean to me. They want to take my mother's house away from me," he moaned. Then eagerly he added, "You said you could help me. I don't want to leave my home."

"Look around Andrew," she directed him. "You're not doing very well living here by yourself. Your mother's house is dirty. The outside has trash everywhere. I don't know," she said to lead him on. "Your mother wouldn't be very happy that you let her house become such a bad place."

Tears started to fill his eyes. This house was the only place he knew. He felt safe in this house, surrounded by his mother's things. "Can you help me please," he begged. "I don't want to go anywhere."

Michele had successfully maneuvered him right where she wanted him. Now she just needed to close the deal. "Do you really want me to help you?"

"Yes, yes, please."

"I can help you, but you'll need to do everything I tell you," she directed. She pretended to think for a couple of minutes. "Let me see. What could I do that will keep the police doctors away. What could I do ....?"

Andrew waited. He was focused on watching Nurse Rice so hard that he had forgotten to breathe. "What, what? Tell me what."

"What would you say if I moved in here with you and I became the mother of the house?"

Andrew's eyes sprung wide open when he heard Michele's plan. "You'd do that for me!" he exclaimed in pure delight.

"It's not going to be easy," she cautioned. "You're going to have to do a lot of hard work to clean this whole house up, from top to bottom so your mother would be proud of you."

"I'll do it. I'll do anything you say. Will you cook the meals and can we do toasts and play games?"

"We'll do everything your mother would do if she were here." Michele answered reassuringly. She was very pleased with herself. Although the last couple of days had been worrisome, today had turned out even better than she could have imagined. She looked around and began forming a list in her head. '*My house is going to be just perfect*' she thought to herself. As for Andrew … she knew she could handle him for the time being.

Chapter 20

Dr. Bevan was perplexed. This morning when she turned on her office computer to read her e-mails there was one that she certainly didn't expect to find. Buried amongst the usual barrage from companies trying to sell her their '*New and Improved'* medical devices, there was a short, to the point e-mail with the heading showing it was from the St. Luke's Hospital, Office of the Director of Nursing.

"Marjorie, can you tell Jason I need to see him?" she called out to her assistant.

She tried to think back. In all her recent discussions with her Investigator, he never mentioned anything remotely like what Doris Hopkins claimed in her note. Although, she did remember that Jason had indicated he had a so called '*Strange Vibe*' feeling about the Hopkins woman.

"You wanted to see me?" Jason asked while he stood in her doorway with his cup of morning coffee dangling from his hand.

"Come in and close the door," Marianne directed.

Jason was uncomfortable with her request to 'close the door'. Lately, with all of the Doctor's overtures towards him, he felt better if the door was left wide open. He was having enough of a struggle in his life dealing with Sergeant Reindle, he didn't want to have to ward off advances from his boss.

"I said, close the door," this time with a firm, 'don't argue with me' tone in her voice.

With the door closed, Jason made a point of moving one of the office chairs to create a safe space between him and the Doctor.

"I want you to take a look at this e-mail I received this morning from Doris Hopkins," she instructed as she passed a printout of the e-mail to Jason.

Jason read the note, then read it again. "I don't understand. Why would that woman write something like this?"

Marianne watched her Investigator's face, looking for any tell-tale sign to show. "That's what I want to know. She states you arrived at her office, pretending to be on official business from me, when in fact she claims what you were really there for was to harass and spy on one of her nurses. When she followed up with her nurse, she learned that you had dated the nurse, but when the nurse rebuffed you, you started stalking her. She's ordering me to direct you to put an end to your unwanted advances or she will be forced to report both you and me to the State Medical Board."

Jason did have a feeling that something wasn't quite right with the Hopkins woman, but he certainly wasn't expecting anything like this. This was so far out in left field that he didn't know what to say to his boss. "You can't possibly believe any of this?" he uttered in disbelief. "I went to the woman's office and asked questions about that Nurse Rice, just as you directed me to do. Nothing else, it was all above board and proper."

"Are you sure that was all you did?" Bevan inquired. "I've seen how you behave whenever you're around that Police Sergeant. How do I know there aren't other women you're tied up with? This is a very serious accusation. I can't just brush off something like this coming from a '*Director of Nursing*' of one the largest hospitals in the region."

Jason was losing his temper. "You leave Claire out of this. I know you have some sort of 'old woman fantasy' and it has to stop. I've taken about all I can stand about your attacks against Claire and me."

Marianne sat back and never uttered a word. She wanted Jason to get all his frustrations out so she could get to the truth about the Hopkin's note.

"And as for this note," he waved the piece of paper wildly in the air. "If you don't believe that I can do my job as a professional, then you should fire me!"

Jason started to get up from his chair to leave. "Sit down," she commanded. "We're not done with this."

Jason sat back down and glared at his boss.

"I believe you, but I needed to be sure. It's obvious what is going on here. Right from the time that Nurse Rice testified at the Blatchford inquest, I recognized her as being a master of manipulation. I just don't know what she's attempting to do." Marianne never responded to Jason's anger over his relationship with Claire. It was better to let that pass for now. "The question I have now is, what do I do with this?"

"I warned you about Hopkins. Why don't you just throw the note in the garbage where it belongs?" Jason answered.

Marianne had been around long enough and was savvy enough to know she couldn't do as Jason had suggested. She knew if she ignored the note, it would come back and bite both Jason and her in the ass. There had to be a way to kill this accusation without it blowing up and ending up spread across the front page of the local paper or possibly even in court. The more she thought about it the more certain she was that Nurse Rice was behind this. She needed to bring some heat onto Rice. "Do you think you can get your Sergeant friend to apply some pressure onto Rice? You don't have to tell her anything about this note. Just tell her that you and I have been talking about what's going on over at St. Luke's and we believe Nurse Rice is hiding something. Something she desperately doesn't want to be made public."

*****

From her office desk, Claire had an unobstructed view of the elevators. When the elevator doors opened, she saw him. She watched as he walked towards her office with a swagger in his step and a smile on his face. To an outside observer, they might think Jason didn't have a care in the world, but as far as Claire was concerned, today was not the day to be smiling. The events of her failed romantic dinner were still too raw in her memory. During her sleepless nights, between bouts of uncontrollable tears, it had slowly come to her. She realized that although she was deeply in love with Jason, he really wasn't in love with her. How could he possibly be in love with her when he had abandoned her to rush off to Bevan. She had worked hard to prepare a sensual dinner complete with glasses of wine and her surprise red lingerie. In return, all Jason could do was to give her a quick peck of a kiss on her cheek as he rushed out of her door. Well damn it, that wasn't enough.

With a quick glance around him to see that no one was watching, "Hi baby," he playfully whispered from her doorway. Claire ignored the greeting and never moved. She kept her head down as she pretended to be engrossed in reading a report that lay on her desk in front of her. Jason thought she didn't hear him, so he walked into the office and stopped directly in front of her. "Claire," he said, this time louder.

Claire slowly looked up. "Oh, it's you. What are you doing here? I'm really busy," she said as she went back to her pretend reading.

Jason could feel the coldness in her voice. The sudden chill that came over him, set him back for a moment. This was so unlike her. Normally she'd be excited to see him. Her face would flush, her eyes would sparkle and if they were alone, she'd be eager to embrace him. "Are you having a bad day?" he asked innocently.

That was too much for Claire. "Is that all you can say, '*Am I having a bad day?*'." She stared hard at him. "No, I'm not having a bad day. What I am having is second thoughts about you."

The violent outburst that Claire fired on Jason caused him to inadvertently take a step backwards. "Where is this coming from?" he asked in amazement. "What in the world has gotten you so riled up?" Taking a moment to think, "Is it something I've done? Whatever it is let's talk about it," he offered trying to calm the wildness that was unfolding in front of him.

"I'm growing tired of being taken for granted. I thought we were in a relationship, but clearly I was mistaken. You're only interested in me when you're not busy with that ridiculous obsession you have with that bitch, Bevan." The vileness in her voice even surprised her. She didn't like talking like this, but enough was enough. This was his last chance, if he truly cared for her, to fight back. To tell her he loved her, and more importantly to start showing it. She needed to be first, not some afterthought. If he didn't make the effort now to show her, it was over.

Claire started and all the anguish that was built up inside of her poured out. " … and I made you dinner … I even bought special wine … you ran out to go to Bevan …" Her sobs were making it hard for Jason to understand her.

"Wait, slow down," he replied to her torment she was pouring out at him. "If I've hurt you, I'm really sorry. I thought you understood. Didn't we both agree that we needed to find the serial killer that's running loose at St. Luke's?"

"Yes."

"Well, that's all I'm trying to do. I know it might seem that I'm being hard on you, but we need to focus on getting this killer before we can think of anything else. The sooner we bring an end to this, the sooner we can move on with our lives together, I promise," he stated.

"And what about Dr. Bevan?"

Jason gave a chuckle. "You have nothing to fear there. It's me that has to watch out for her."

“You mean it?” she asked, looking for some reassurance that he wasn’t just talking.

Jason walked around the desk, lifted Claire from her chair, embraced her and kissed her with a slow, warm, moist kiss. “I really do mean it.”

From outside the office, Detective Morrison had watched the lover soap opera. When he had seen his Sergeant break down in tears, he just about rushed into her office to support her. Now, seeing how the show had ended he was glad he didn’t. “You two should get a room,” he called out in jest.

Both Jason and Claire blushed. “I really have got to start closing doors,” Jason mumbled to himself.

Chapter 21

In her office, Dr. Bevan studied the toxicology report she had just received from the lab. She knew what she was looking for had to be buried here somewhere in the mess of numbers in front of her. When she had completed the autopsy on Myron Crowley, there was nothing unusual that stood out. All she found were the normal tell-tale signs of a senior who had lived his life with little regard for his health. The liver had showed the hardening you'd expect to find in someone who was more than just a social drinker. The lungs had displayed the black early signs of scarring from long term smoking. And the prostrate, well, she could tell that was a time bomb that was just waiting to go off. But she knew none of these things were responsible for Crowley's sudden, untimely death. The answer had to be in the lab report.

As part of her search for the 'Death Angel', she had issued an order to St. Luke's Hospital, that she was to be personally notified of every death that occurred before any remains were released to the grieving family. After a quick review of the notices she had recently received, she had let them all pass. They didn't have the red flags she was watching for. They weren't men. They weren't seniors and they weren't from the hospital's fourth floor.

When she received the notice detailing Mr. Crowley's passing, it was different from the rest. It carried all the warning signs. Crowley was male, senior, and from the hospital fourth floor. She immediately issued a 'Hold' on the body. A scan of the hospital medical records showed that Mr. Crowley had been given 2 x 10mg tablets of Temazepam, supposedly to relieve the patient's restless anxiety and aid in his sleep. And surprise, surprise, the Doctor thought to herself. The nurse who had administered the tablets was none other than Nurse Michele Rice. The clincher was that the toxicology report showed there was a buildup of ten times the amount of Temazepam in the body's system than what was recorded in the medical charts. She had found it. There was more than enough Temazepam in Crowley's system to induce a deep, permanent sleep.

Dr. Bevan thought for a long moment. With all that was going on, she wanted to make sure she did not only the right thing, but also that her actions were the smart thing to be doing. She decided there was no point in holding an inquest. She didn't need an inquest to tell her Mr. Crowley's death was clearly an 'Angel' death. Nor did she need an inquest to tell her that everything about Mr. Crowley's untimely passing pointed towards Nurse Rice.

Her investigator, Alder, had reported back to her that he had completed the last instruction she had given him. After a surprise heated heart to heart with Claire, he had informed her of the concerns the doctor had about Nurse Rice trying to hide something. As a result of that information, Claire had promised to send her two detectives out to interview the suspect nurse. When Bevan had heard back from the police, she was disappointed. The interview had turned out to be fruitless. Rice had proven herself to be too clever for the inept detectives. So now she had to make a decision. Did she send Jason back to Reindle with more information that she knew Claire really should know, or did she take matters into her own hands and tell the police sergeant herself? Besides, she felt it wasn't her responsibility to continually drive Jason back into the arms of the lovesick Police Sergeant, Claire Reindle. Although she didn't like it, she decided she was going to have to tell Reindle personally.

*****

She hoped the hot water from her morning shower would help to revive her. Even though her day hadn't yet started, she was already tired. It had been a long, restless night for the Doctor where dreams of men, all wearing torn hospital gowns as shrouds haunted her. They kept calling out, over and over again, '*Help me, help me*'.

Hot water poured over her, splashing away at the soap lather while she scrubbed harder and harder as in some vain attempt to flush the wrinkled lines that snaked across her body down the shower drain. Already she knew it wasn't going to be a good day.

Finally, out of the shower, freshly dried off, she stood naked in front of her bathroom mirror and examined herself. The reflected old woman that looked back at her confirmed what she already knew. Her breasts, which were once full and firm, with cleavage that drew admiring stares wherever she went, now sagged, lifeless towards the floor. Her growing stomach paunch showed the results of her poor eating habits. On the counter, her hairbrush lay filled with a tangled mass of gray strands of hair. All the expensive shampoos and fancy promising conditioners she had tried couldn't stop the daily loss of hair that plagued her. Looking in the mirror she took it all in. She could hide most of it. Clothes, make-up, coloring all played an important role in her disguise. But her hands! Nothing could hide her hands. No matter how hard she tried, it was her hands that screamed out to her that she was old.

*****

Sitting in the back seat of the car, with her briefcase, stuffed full of the suspected 'Angel' medical files, resting beside her, she was ready. Dr. Bevan had her assistant, Marjorie, drive her across the city, through the chaos of morning rush hour traffic, to the Police

Services Building. When she stepped from the car, her empty stomach, slightly queasy from the drive, gurgled. "Thank you, Marjorie," she said in embarrassment. "This shouldn't take too long; can you please pick me up in an hour?" Although it wasn't in her job description to drive around the city as the Doctor's personal chauffeur, Marjorie didn't mind. It gave her some free time to get out of her stuffy office and enjoy the outside air.

Bevan didn't like having to leave her office to report her findings directly to Sergeant Reindle, but she could see no other way. The killings were getting out of control and the information she now had could have a large impact on the police investigation.

Wearing a camel-colored skirt which fell to the perfect length of one inch below her knees, along with an emerald green top, she was dressed a little more upscale than she normally would have been if she was staying in her own office. Filled with confidence, she approached the reception desk, "Could you direct me to the office of Sergeant Reindle please?"

The aged officer behind the protective glass shield had been around long enough that he recognized the Doctor. "Dr. Bevan, it's good to see you." He was curious as to why she had ventured outside of her office, but he decided it would be wise not to ask. For as long as he could remember, rumours had circulated throughout the force that the Doctor rarely left the confines of her office. Whatever had brought her here must be of some importance he surmised.

“Is Sergeant Reindle expecting you?” he asked.

“I shouldn’t think so,” Marianne chuckled. It was bad enough that she had to travel across the city to get to Sergeant Reindle’s office, there was no way she was going to lower herself to the point of phoning to make an appointment.

After a needless security check, the Doctor was led to the elevators. “Sergeant Reindle will meet you on the sixth floor.” Inside the closed elevator, Marianne straightened her skirt, then took a couple of deep breaths to prepare herself for what she believed had the potential to be a very uncomfortable meeting.

When Claire was told that Dr. Bevan was in the elevator on her way up to see her, she grimaced to herself. But this was her home turf, she thought. And, if Bevan decided to get testy, well, she was more than confidant she could hold her own against this woman any day of the week.

“Dr. Bevan, this is a pleasant surprise,” Claire greeted. She was clearly wearing a forced smile, but unable to hide the dripping sarcasm from her voice. “What in the world could possibly have brought you here?”

Marianne didn’t want to beat around the bush by wasting time exchanging false pleasantries. She looked Claire straight in the eyes, "There's been another one!"

Claire was surprised by Bevan's comment. It was a comment that had caused the Sergeant's eyes to show a spark of intrigue. "Perhaps we should go to my office then?" Claire offered.

Inside the Sergeant's office the two women eyed each other. One was upset with the continued interference the other caused in her personal life. One was unhappy with the impact the other had on her fantasy dreams. But for now, those feelings had to be put aside. They both had a job to do. Dr. Bevan was eager to turn over the information she carried so she could return to the comfort of her own office as quickly as she could.

"What do you mean '*There's been another one*'? Claire asked.

Bevan took a deep breath. She knew she was going to have to take her time explaining her findings to Claire. " ... Mr. Crowley died unexpectantly ... I performed an autopsy and found there was no physical reason for him to die ... A toxicology report showed he had been given a massive dose of Temazepam."

The Sergeant had been busily taking notes of everything Bevan was telling her. "Hold on for a minute," she paused the Doctor. "What's Temazepam?"

"It's a drug that when given in small doses reduces anxiety, relaxes the body and aids in allowing sleep. But when given in such a large dose, as Crowley was given, it leads to a long, permanent sleep," Bevan explained.

"So," Claire summarized what the Doctor had told her. "We now have four confirmed 'Angel' deaths."

"Oh my dear," Marianne's motherly voice chimed. "I'm afraid there's a lot more than just four." Bevan stood up from her chair, opened her briefcase, and dumped the files in the center of the Sergeant's desk.

"What's all this?"

"These are the medical records from St. Luke's Hospital that I believe are all linked to the actions of our so called 'Death Angel'."

Claire took a moment and read off a couple of the names written on the files. "Tylee, Wilson, Higginson, McFarlane. My God! How many are there? Why didn't we know about these?" she asked in disbelief.

"To answer your first question," the Doctor began. "There's far too many. And as to why we didn't know of these, that's easy. Dr. Coleus had been falsifying the weekly Mortality Reports for the last two months."

"You're saying all these have happened in only the last two months?" Looking at the pile on her desk, she found it hard to believe.

"Yes. And there's more you need to know," Bevan stated. "I've studied all these medical records and have arrived with a couple of crucial facts."

"Like what?" Claire asked with her pencil ready to write.

"First, the victims are all senior men from the hospital's fourth floor who died during the night. Now, I've had my Investigator, Jason, do a cross check against the hospital employee night work schedule. For every one of these deaths, he's found that the Nurse Michele Rice, was the lead nurse on duty, on the fourth floor of the hospital, at that time."

Claire stopped writing. "I've had my detectives interview Nurse Rice, as Jason had suggested, and there's nothing solid we can pin on her. If she is the 'Angel' she's very clever. There's so many people travelling through that fourth floor on any given night, that all we have is circumstantial evidence. It could be anyone of them."

"Ahh, but here's something you don't know," the Doctor stated, quite proud of herself. "The medical record of Myron Crowley clearly shows that Nurse Rice admitted giving him 'Temazepam' on the night he was killed."

Claire thought for a moment. "You're sure of this?"

"It's all recorded in the medical records."

The Sergeant's mind was racing. She believed this could be the solid evidence that she needed to lay charges against Michele Rice. "Dr. Bevan, I owe you for this," she declared. "We'll pick up Rice immediately and begin the process of laying formal charges against her." Then she thought for a moment. "And Dr. Coleus. By him falsifying those Mortality Reports, he was enabling the killings to go on without being detected. We can charge him with being complicit in the murders."

"I've no doubt that Rice is harboring some deep secret she doesn't want exposed. But, to return the favor, I'd like to ask you to hold off on laying any charges against Coleus. Leave him to me. When I'm done with him, I'll turn him over to you."

Marianne rose from her chair and began stuffing the medical files back into her briefcase.

"You know, maybe I've had you all wrong," Claire muttered under her breath.

When Marianne heard Claire, it struck a nerve with her. She put down her briefcase and sat back down. What she was about to say was too heavy to say standing up. "Strange you should say that. Being here and talking with you makes me realize we're a lot alike."

The sincerity in Bevan's voice surprised Claire. She never expected to hear the Doctor say things like '*They were a lot alike.*' If anything, Claire thought, they were miles apart on just about everything. "I don't understand. Why would you say that?"

Marianne leaned back in her chair, crossed her hands in her lap and drifted. "Oh, I know physically we are vastly different. You're young, full of life while I on the other hand am growing older and have become very set in my ways."

Claire watched the Doctor. From the look on her face and the calmness in her eyes, she appeared to be very much at peace with herself. Claire had never seen Bevan like this. Normally whenever she was around the Doctor, she always appeared stiff, sharp and would be constantly snipping at her. This was a whole new side of Bevan.

Marianne continued with her musing. "I was once young and beautiful like you," she said as she looked down at her tell-tale hands. "I too thought I was in love with a handsome, kind man. He showered me with gifts and promised me a future where we would travel and see the world. We were set to cruise off to Hawaii on a whirl-wind tour of romance and adventure, before I realized the truth. He was in love with a ghost. A past love that had a hold on him that he simply couldn't and didn't want to let go of. Although he never realized it and I'm sure he never intended it, he was using me in an attempt to relive the joy of a past life that he could no longer have."

The sadness of Bevan's story struck Claire deeper than she realized.

"I know you think you are in love with my investigator, Jason. He's handsome, virile and has the ability to draw you to him whenever the mood strikes him. As an old woman, I also feel myself being drawn to him. But I confess, that it's because I'm lonely. My fantasy is all I have besides my work. And I do realize it's just a fantasy," she sighed. "But that fantasy keeps me warm and makes me feel as if I am alive."

The frankness of the Doctor amazed Claire. The openness with which she shared her feelings felt like a weight bearing down on her. She had a lot of thinking to do. Maybe her love for Jason wasn't real. Maybe she was trying to change him when he couldn't be changed. Her saucer brown eyes began to moisten. When she looked towards Marianne, she saw that the Doctor's piercing blue eyes had also begun to moisten.

Bevan quietly rose from her chair. With her briefcase securely tucked under her arm, "We'll talk soon," she promised as she left the Sergeant's office.

*****

The noise that suddenly came from her door startled Michele as she sat on her hair covered couch. Her cats annoyingly scratched away on the couch's worn arm rests. She had been busily making herself a list of all the things that needed to be done in preparation to move into Andrew's home. Originally, she had thought she would simply hire a cleaning company to go through the house from top to bottom and make a clean sweep of the entire place. A quick check into the price of hiring cleaners told her that was out of the question. She found out cleaners made as much if not more than she made as a nurse. She didn't have the money to pay for them and she wasn't fully sure of Andrew's money situation just yet. And that was another thing she needed to add onto her growing list of things to be done.

When she opened her door, she instantly recognized the two detectives. The size of the pair made them hard to forget. "You, again? You were just here. What do you want now?"

Detective Swan's lower lip inadvertently curled up as he remembered, from their past visits, the sour cat odour that crept out from inside the woman's apartment.

Detective Morrison took the lead. "Ms. Rice, we have a few more questions we need to ask you. May we come in?"

The two detectives were following up on the latest orders given to them from their Sergeant. After what at first had started out to be a tense one on one between the Sergeant and Doctor Bevan, Claire learned of the Doctor's concerns about the nurse, Michele Rice. Although she wasn't happy to be doing Marianne's bidding, when she thought about it, it made sense. Since the orderly, Andrew Brompton, had been deemed to be incapable of committing the complicated murders at the hospital, why not a trained nurse? If Nurse Rice was hiding a secret, as Dr. Bevan suspected, then it was worth investigating to find out what it was.

Detective Swan started to move forward, but Michele never moved and stood blocking his way. "I'm really busy right now," she declared. "I'm afraid you'll have to come back another time." Michele moved in a failed attempt to close her door.

"Ms. Rice. We are now investigating a multiple murder case and it's important we ask you a few questions," Tony stated.

Detective Swan wasn't as polite as his partner. "You can either answer our questions now or you can get your coat and accompany us to the station. The choice is yours."

Michele reluctantly stepped back to allow the two to enter as her cats moved forward to greet their two new playthings.

'Meowww' Mr. Briggs, the cat, wailed. Detective Swan, not being a cat lover had inadvertently stepped on the cat's tail. He tried to hold back the grin as he apologized, "I'm sorry, I didn't see the cat there."

Once they were seated on the lone couch in Michele's living room area, Tony took out his pad and pencil.

"Ms. Rice, When we last talked, we discussed the sudden deaths of a Mr. Bittman, and a Mr. Blatchford."

Swan added into the mix, "And don't forget about Haughton."

Michele was on her guard and didn't want to admit to anything no matter how simple the question appeared to be. "Like I told you then, of course I know of Mr. Blatchford. I attended the inquest that was held for him." Then thinking, "And oh yes. I remember you two asking questions about the Bittman death that started from some note you had received. But I remember nothing about a Haughton. To my knowledge nothing has changed. For the most part I just do my work and don't pay attention to any of the gossip that constantly floats around the hospital."

Detective Morrison continued. "Recently a lot has changed," he corrected her. "More deaths have come to light including the most recent death of a Myron Crowley. Another one of your patients who your very own medical records show you personally administered the drug," Tony checked his notepad, "Temazepam."

Michele stopped and thought for a moment. "I'm sorry to hear about Mr. Crowley. Yes, you're right. I do remember giving Mr. Crowley 2 x 10mg tablets of Temazepam as was prescribed by Dr. Coleus. Mr.

Crowley was very agitated and needed the medicine to help him sleep."

Detective Swan quickly piped in, "The so-called medicine you gave to him did a lot more than help him sleep, it killed him!"

"That's impossible," Michele shot back in defence. "I administered the exact dosage as prescribed."

"Ms. Rice. When we began to check into these deaths one thing stood out," Tony stated. "The Medical Examiner has determined that all of these deaths occurred on the same hospital ward. And," Tony continued, "what makes it even more interesting is they all happened at or around the time that you were working on that ward. So, you can see why we need to talk with you. Can you explain how all these deaths have a common link to you?"

Michele now found herself in a spot. She had already attempted to use Andrew to divert any attention away from her, but that didn't work. She had successfully lied to Doris about why the Medical Investigator, Jason, was asking questions about her background. But now with the police focusing in on her, she was quickly running out of tales to tell.

"Well obviously it's little more than a terrible coincidence. There are dozens of people that work on the ward every night. Any one of them could be the one you are looking for. I work damn hard every night and am respected by my fellow nurses and doctors alike. I'm insulted that you or anyone would think that I could be capable of harming any of the patients in my care."

The two detectives took turns rapidly firing off an endless string of questions in the hope she would get confused and slip up in the story she was telling them. But Michele never wavered. She wasn't the type of woman that got easily flustered, even when she was being bullied by two oversized gorillas.

*****

When they returned to the Police Department, Swan and Morrison headed directly to the Sergeant's Office. "Sarge, have you got a minute?" Julian asked from her doorway.

Claire motioned for the two to come in. "What's up?"

"It's Rice. We were just at her apartment questioning her as you wanted and it didn't go well."

Claire stopped what she was doing. "Did you hit her with Crowley and the Temazepam?"

"Yea"

"And did you tell her we have the medical records that show her as being the one who administered the drug?"

"Yea"

“Well then, what’s the problem?”

Tony took over the story. “We hit her with everything you told us. We questioned her back and forth for over an hour and she never faltered once. She stuck to her story of administering the exact dosage as prescribed by Coleus. She claimed that Crowley was monitored by both her and her partner during the night and was found to be sleeping peacefully. No matter what we tried, we couldn’t get her to slip up. Not once,” he stated.

The Sergeant paused for a moment as she attempted to take it all in. “I don’t know about you two, but I’ve had just about enough of playing with this woman. Send a ‘Black and White’ over to her apartment to pick her up. Tell them to put some cuffs on her and put her in one of the cells downstairs for the night. We’ll see if that will shake her up. Dr. Bevan believes all these deaths revolve around Rice, and I tend to agree with her.”

“You know she’s going to scream blue murder!”

“Let her. The Commissioner has called and says he wants to see me. I’ll brief him on what we’re doing. We can hold her as a ‘Person of Interest’ for 72 hours,” Claire declared.

Chapter 22

She stood quietly in front of the large imposing desk and waited for the Commissioner to acknowledge her. He was busily scribbling his signature on a number of forms that needed to be signed. Claire noticed that today he was wearing a blue bow tie to match his blue jacket. She wondered if the matching bow tie was his choice or was it something his wife made him wear. Either way it gave him a distinctive look.

Finally putting his pen down, he turned his attention towards her. "Sergeant Reindle." The tone of his voice reminded Claire of the times she stood in front of her high school Principal, years ago, when she would receive so called '*Helpful*' advice on how a lady was supposed to act. "I'm glad you're here. I was wondering when you were going to get around to give me an update. It's been some time and I haven't heard from you on any progress you've made."

"Commissioner, I'm sorry, but we have been very busy. This is the first chance I've had some free time. I have filed my regular reports," Claire said in her defence.

"I've read them. And I can tell you I'm disturbed with what I've been reading."

"Again, I'm sorry, but this case has blown up far bigger than the original 'Bittman' note you gave me." Claire could tell that he was happy that he had been right about the 'Bittman' note being real and that she had been wrong, even though he never really showed it. If it had of been her that was right, and the note had proven to be nothing more than a waste of time, she wouldn't have hesitated to tell him '*I told you so*'.

"I need to be honest with you," he started. "I realize you're relatively new here and haven't been in your position for very long." He paused, as he tried to figure out the best way to tell the Sergeant of his concerns. "I'm wondering if this case might be just a little too big for you to effectively handle. Maybe it needs someone who's more experienced to lead the investigation."

Claire was shocked to hear the threat from the Commissioner. She expected that she might get a dressing down, but she never expected to hear him say that he was thinking of replacing her. Was it that he had concerns about her leadership skills or was this a move to put a man in the lead because he thought the case was simply too complicated to have a woman in charge. She knew she had to handle this, but she had to stay cool. It would do her no good to get upset or to get all '*Womanly*' in front of Baywright.

Claire took a breath to steady herself. "Commissioner, I admit this case has had it's share of difficulties."

Baywright interrupted her, "Difficulties or excuses?"

Claire ignored the obvious jab. "We've had to deal with a tightly knit medical system that has opposed us every step of the way. And we've had to work, hand in hand, with the feisty Medical Examiner, Dr. Bevan, which in itself hasn't been easy. But in spite of these hurdles, I'm happy to say, my team and I have been making steady progress."

"Ahh, Dr. Bevan," he chuckled. "I can sympathize with you there. Over the years I've had more than my share of face-to-face battles with the woman. It was never easy," he remembered, "but more often than not, she always proved herself to be more of a help than a hinderance."

Claire decided it would serve no purpose to mention that he never had to deal with Bevan over any kind of a love relationship as she had to do. But, since her last meeting in her office with the doctor, she felt they had finally come to a fragile working connection.

He held up his hand, "Wait a minute," he said. He called over his desk intercom, "Nancy, can you bring me the 'Bittman' file please."

When Nancy came in and deposited the file on the desk, she gave Claire a subtle look that Claire interpreted as ‘Good Luck’.

“Now let’s see,” he muttered as he began to turn the pages of the file. “You started out by looking into possible criminal reasons for Bittman suddenly dying. Humm… You now indicate that you’re looking into four cases. That’s quite a jump, wouldn’t you say?”

“Those are all suspicious deaths that we have uncovered going on over at St. Luke’s Hospital,” she replied. She never mentioned that in fact, according to Dr. Bevan, there were considerably more deaths that needed to be looked into.

“Well, as I read in your reports here, what have you done other than interview a number of people. With four confirmed deaths, I would have expected some sort of action by now. But I don’t see any.”

When he put it that way, even Claire thought he was right. What exactly had she done? The ‘Angel’ was still free to operate however and as often as it pleased. In a panic she had to think of something …

“Working with the Organized Crime Group, we have uncovered that the Head of the Hospital Cardiac Unit has been involved in a scheme of Bribery and Kick Backs using Public Funds,” she blurted out with the hope that highlighting the possibility of the surfacing of a blatant case of Public Corruption might do her some good.

Baywright looked at her and shook his head. "I didn't ask about that. This is exactly what I've been talking about. Not being focused. You're in Homicide, not Organized Crime. Leave that to them. You can't afford to be wasting either you or your detectives time when you have a mass killer active. I want to know what you have done to stop the killings?"

Claire was getting frustrated. She could see no way out of this. "It's not that easy. We don't know who the killer is. The killings appear to be happening at random, so there's nothing we can grab hold of. The one suspect we uncovered that had a motive to possibly be the killer turned out to be mentally incapable of committing the crimes. But, working with Dr. Bevan, we have now identified a prime 'Person of Interest' who we are holding in the cells right now, trying to shake her up."

Baywright leaned back, "At least that's something. You can hold her for 72 hours. By that time you should know one way or the other whether or not she is your killer. But," he stated, while staring directly into the Sergeant's eyes, "and this is a pretty big but. If I don't see some real action in the next while, I'll be forced to replace you and your whole team. I can't sit by and continue to let these killings go on. Am I making myself clear?"

"Crystal."

"Alright, get out of here and do your job, not everyone else's. I don't care how you do it, but you need to make things happen!"

When Claire arrived back at her office, she collapsed in her chair. Everything about her, her body, the way she sat, the way her face drooped, told anyone who was looking her way, that she was defeated.

*****

Detective Morrison stopped what he was doing. His partner, Swan, was standing in front of his desk, acting giddy as a child who had just captured a frog.

"What's gotten into you?"

"We've got him!" Detective Swan declared. His eyes were bright and his face was flushed with excitement. He was overjoyed with the plan he had worked out. Unfortunately, unknown to him, it was the exact plan that his Sergeant had attempted to use when she tried, in a failed attempt, to save her skin from the beating the Commissioner laid on her.

Tony looked puzzled but waited for Julian to explain.

"I've met with the boys over in the 'Organized Crime Group'."

"Yeah, and?" Tony tried to edge the information out of his partner.

"Remember those unexplained chunks of money that appeared in Coleus's bank records? It turns out the OC group has been watching an engineering company going by the name of 'Franco Construction & Engineering'. This company is the one that has been involved with the expansion project going on over at St. Luke's. Now stay with me," Julian continued. " … Franco is owned by a numbered company financed by none other than George Logan."

"You mean the Logan who's the kingpin of the drug and racketeering action going on in the state?"

"Exactly," Swan could barely contain himself. "And it gets even better."

With the mention of the name 'Logan', Swan had his partner's undivided attention.

"Through Mayor Shultz, the St. Luke's Expansion has received several sizeable grants of city money. If they can prove that the money in Coleus's bank account came from Franco Engineering, Coleus could be facing anywhere from 5 to 10 years on public bribery and corruption charges.

Tony thought for a moment, "And how exactly do you plan to prove that?"

"Easy. They plan on making him a deal. They have it worked out that if he turns state's evidence against Franco Engineering, the OC guys will drop the bribery charges involving public funds. The Organized Crime

Guys are excited. After years of trying, they see a chance on finally getting Logan."

"The Sergeant will never go for that," Morrison stated. "It would mean Dr. Coleus would get off scot free."

"No. No. Here's the best part. I've already gone ahead and talked with that Medical Investigator, Adler. He says the Medical Examiner's Office is putting together a case to go before the State Medical Licencing Board to have Coleus's Medical Licence stripped from him. Without his licence Coleus would have nothing. He'd be put out on the street and never be allowed to practice medicine again."

"Well, even with that, I doubt if the Sergeant would go for this," Tony mused. "You know she's made some kind of deal between herself and Dr. Bevan. Don't you remember? She's already told us to stay away from anything involving Coleus."

"Yea," Swan replied. "But that doesn't make any sense. The OC Group will get Logan and Coleus will be put out of business. It doesn't get any better than that!"

Tony mused, "The Sergeant might not like it, but you know who would be really happy?"

"No. Who?"

"That crazy nurse Lucy Spencer!"

*****

Detective Morrison sat back and let his partner, Detective Swan, take the lead. Tony had decided that until he knew which way his Sergeant was going to go, it was better for him to take a back seat to his partner. Lately, he had noticed the increased animosity that had grown between his Sergeant and the Medical Examiner, Dr. Bevan, had mellowed. It used to be that any time Dr. Bevan's name would come up, the Sergeant's face would turn sour. But now, the expected sour face had been replaced by an ever so slight grin.

In the Sergeant's office, Julian had ramped up, well into his explanation. "It's simple. Everything falls into place. The Organized Crime Group, gets Logan, so they're happy. Dr. Bevan gets Coleus, so she's happy. Everybody wins."

It took all the effort that Claire could muster to contain the anger building up inside of her. At her recent meeting with the Commissioner, he had made it perfectly clear to her that her job depended on her being able to put an end to the hospital killings. He wasn't the least bit interested in hearing anything about the work of the Organized Crime Group from her.

Tony could visibly see the red flush as it rose up across Claire's face.

With a voice, steel cold through clamped teeth, “And what about the ‘Angel’ murders that are happening at the hospital?” she asked. “You’ve been so busy patting yourself on the back for doing everyone else’s job, you haven’t been doing your own!”

Swan slunk back in his chair. Unlike his partner, he never expected this amount of animosity from the Sergeant. He had been so happy with his plan that he anticipated hearing sounds of applause, a celebrational parade around the office, maybe even a cake for him to slice. Swan looked over to his partner. Tony could see the desperate look in Julian’s eyes that pleaded, ‘Help me please!’

Not knowing that the Sergeant’s job, and his job for that matter, were on the line, he piped in to try and rescue his partner. “Come on Sarge. Don’t you think you’re being a little unfair? After all, we’re going to get Logan and maybe put a sizeable dent in his whole crime operation along with forcing Dr. Coleus out. That’s not bad,” he said.

Claire turned her attention to Morrison. “What is it with you two? I agree with what you say. Those are both good things. Don’t you think I’ve already thought of that?” The words of the Commissioner that were still bouncing around in her brain, came back to her. “But you two have to get it through your thick heads, we work in Homicide!” There was a touch of desperation in her voice. “We have a growing list of confirmed murders that we need to solve. It looks to me that you've forgotten there's a suspected serial killer running amuck at St. Luke's? I would think that's what we should be concentrating on?"

"We never said we were quitting," Tony tried to reason. "We're going to get the killer."

Claire had heard more than she could take. "Alright, enough," she relented. "That's all I can take. Now for 'Pete's Sake', please, lets focus on finding the killer and forget about everything else. You have our Prime Suspect, Rice, sitting downstairs in the cells and neither one of you have done anything with her." Claire was at the point of nearly pleading with her detectives. "Time is running out. Start doing your jobs and get rattling her cage. We need for her to make a mistake and give us a confession!"

*****

After a long talk with Detective Swan, Jason decided he had better run the Detective's plan past his boss. "Can I talk with you for a minute?" he asked.

Marianne looked up and saw her Investigator standing in her doorway. Seeing him there, after her recent confession to Sergeant Reindle, made her realize how foolish she had been acting. Her past fantasies were now nothing more than that. 'Past Fantasies' of an old lonely woman.

"Come in. I've just been sitting here thinking."

When Jason entered and sat in one of the chairs, he noticed something was different with the Doctor. She didn't appear to have the sparkle in her eyes that she normally had whenever he approached her. "Are you alright?"

'*Yes*', she thought. '*I'm alright. I've been a fool, but now I'm alright'*.

"I'm fine. What is it you want," she said, in a voice that carried the message that she was now all business.

"One of the police detectives, Swan, invited me to have a coffee with him."

"That's nice. And you wanted to tell me this why?"

"He's come up with a plan that he needs our help with." Jason went on to explain the details he had heard from Swan.

Bevan listened intently. When Jason was done, she decided to test her investigator.

"And just what do you think of the Detective's plan."

"I think there's a lot of potential in it. That's why I wanted to run it past you before I committed to doing anything."

Failed!

"I have to say I'm a little disappointed."

Jason didn't understand. To him the plan seemed to have a lot of merit. "Disappointed why?" he asked.

"For a number of reasons," Bevan began. "First of all, if the police want our help to effectively do their job, they need to contact me." The doctor wanted to make sure she asserted that she was the one in charge. "Second. A practicing doctor can not lose his licence for things that do not pertain to his medical actions. It doesn't matter if he's a crook involved in criminal doings. Being a crook has nothing to do with him being a good doctor. And lastly, and probably the most important is something you'll learn with a little more experience."

"And what's that?"

Bevan went on to explain what had taken her years of experience to realize, "The State Medical Licensing Board is an 'Old Boys' club. For us to make a case to have a Doctor's Licence withdrawn we need to have pretty solid, undeniable evidence of 'Medical Incompetence'. We'd need to prove that the Doctor was incapable of performing his duties. Now that's a lot different than 'Medical Malpractice'. Malpractice is looked at as nothing more than a Doctor making a mistake. For that all he'd get would be a sanction, a slap on the wrist or at worst a fine. And remember, with the shortage of practicing physicians in this state, any case we put forward would have to be airtight to be successful."

"So, you're saying we should do nothing," Jason challenged. "We should just let Coleus get away without being held accountable for any of his actions."

Bevan shook her head. It was clear to her that he missed the point of what she was saying. "No. What I'm saying is there's a world of difference between the legal world and the medical world. We need to let the police do what they think is best from a legal standpoint. We, on the other hand, need to concentrate on what we need to do from a medical standpoint." Then she added, "Listen, I want to get Coleus as much as anyone. The difference being that when we go after him, we'll be rock solid and he won't be able to squirm out of it."

*****

In the morning, when Doris Hopkins checked the night time Nursing Shift Reports, she noticed Nurse Rice had failed to show up for her shift. Her shift had been worked by Nurse Berna on an overtime basis. This was so unlike Michele. She had never missed a night's work before, thought Doris. A quick check of the medical records for the last 24 hours showed Michele never came into the Emergency Department as a patient, so she couldn't have been involved in any kind of an accident. If she was sick or had some kind of problem at home, Doris knew she would have called to let her know, after all she felt they were such good friends. She started to worry. Retrieving Michele's phone number, she decided to call.

'Buzz ... Buzz ... Buzz.' 'The number you are calling is not available. At the sound of the beep, record your message' ... 'Beep'

Michele's phone rang unnoticed in the Police property room. There was no one there that was going to answer it.

"Michele, this is Doris. I noticed you weren't at work last night. I hope everything is ok. Please give me a call as soon as you can. I'm worried about you."

With no answer, Doris's anxiety started to rise. She started to pace, back and forth across her office. She was sure something must have happened to her friend. Back and forth, back and forth. Maybe that Jason was pestering her again. Maybe he was holding her captive somewhere. Her mind filled with visions of men and their depravity.

'Buzz ... Buzz ... Buzz.' "Dr. Bevan's Office," the cheerful voice chimed.

"This is Doris Hopkins, Director of Nursing for St. Luke's Hospital, it's important I speak with Dr. Bevan right away."

The call was relayed through to the Doctor. "Bevan here, how can I help you?"

In Doris's mind, all kinds of unseemly deeds had befallen her friend. "I've warned you once before, you need to keep that animal you have working for you away from my Nurse Rice. I'm sure he's gone crazy and has her locked up somewhere. What are you going to do about it?" Doris had worked herself long passed the point of reason. "You need to help her, right now!"

Doctor Bevan listened to the outrageous rant that was sounding in her ear. Clearly Hopkins was having some sort of a breakdown. "Miss Hopkins," the doctor said in a soothing voice. "You need to calm yourself down. Take a couple of deep breaths. I assure you everything is ok. Nurse Rice is in good hands."

"How can you be so sure? You're wasting valuable time, covering up for that Jason," Doris screamed through the phone at the Doctor.

"Right now, Nurse Rice is being held in Police custody. This has absolutely nothing to do with my Investigator Jason Alder."

In police custody! This had turned from bad to worse ... "Why have you done this to her? She's never done anything wrong. That Alder has put you up to this, hasn't he?"

"Nurse Rice is in custody as a 'Person of Interest' concerning the rash of deaths that have occurred on her ward there at the hospital. Now you need to calm down. If she's innocent then the police will release her."

"Of course, she's innocent you damn fool. Michele could never hurt anyone." With that Doris slammed down her phone. Back and forth, back and forth. Each time she passed by her desk she saw the picture of Sampson the cat, his cat, laughing at her. Back and forth, back and forth. She picked up the picture and heaved it, with all her might at the wall.

'*Crash*' shattered glass flew everywhere.

"They're going to pay for this. I'll make sure they pay," Doris muttered.

*****

Michele had never been locked overnight in a cell before, but when she looked around, it didn't seem to be all that much different from being locked in her rundown apartment every day. The cell, although compact, contained everything she needed. There was a wash area, a chair bolted to the floor with a small table and a bed. The only things missing were the ceiling crack above the bed and her cats. She knew her cats would be ok, provided this craziness didn't go on for too long. They were used to having the run of the apartment on the nights when she went to work. If this, by chance, did happen to drag on, she'd have to somehow get word to Andrew and tell him to go pick up the cats.

She was having a difficult time trying to figure out what the police expected to gain by detaining her. As far as she was concerned, being locked up with three free meals a day and being able to get a peaceful night's sleep was a holiday from her normal life. They could hold her for as long as they wanted, it didn't matter. Her story wasn't going to change, neither today nor tomorrow. She was determined to sit back, relax and wait until whoever was in charge came to their senses.

*****

"How's our suspect doing in the cells?" Claire asked Swan.

"I was just talking to the keeper downstairs and he indicated she slept well during the night and wolfed down all of her breakfast this morning."

Hearing the report resulted in Claire feeling an uneasiness start to grow in the pit of her stomach. A lot depended on getting an 'Angel' confession out of Michele. She had been counting on the Nurse to be rattled, upset or at the very least to be angry.

"I think it's time to bring her up and start putting some pressure on her," Claire directed. "So far she hasn't asked for a lawyer. That's a big bonus for us. We need to take advantage of it while we can," she stated. Then she added as a warning, "Remember her 72 hour clock is ticking!"

By the time Michele had been brought up to Interview Room #2, both Morrison and Swan were already settled in their places waiting for her. The recording systems had been activated and tested. When Tony first laid eyes on the woman she wasn't at all like he had expected her to be. To him, she appeared to be fresh, invigorated and confidant. Rattling this woman was not going to be easy he realized.

“Ms. Rice,” Tony began. “I want to remind you that you do have the right to have a lawyer present. If you can not afford a lawyer, one will be appointed, free of charge. Do you understand this right?”

Michele just looked nonchalant towards him. “I don’t think I need a lawyer. And as far as I’m concerned, you people are just wasting your time. I’ve got nothing to hide.” But she did have a secret hidden deep, and so far, only Doctor Bevan had sensed it.

Detectives Morrison and Swan fired questions towards Michele for over two hours, nonstop. The barrage of questions just bounced harmlessly off of Michele. No matter what the question, her answer never changed. They were getting exhausted, but Detective Swan refused to back away. The interview quickly changed into being a battle of wills between the two. After three hours, Tony suddenly called for a stop. He knew that after that amount of nonstop questioning, if any confession had surfaced, it would easily be thrown out of court by any defence lawyer worth his salt.

*****

“I don’t know about this,” Detective Morrison reported to his Sergeant. “We’ve leaned on her pretty heavy but it doesn’t seem to have any effect on her.”

"Yea," added Detective Swan. "We've questioned her for over three hours and it didn't seem to faze her. No matter what or how we ask her she keeps giving us the same answer back. This is one tough woman. I've had hardened criminals crack easier than her."

This was the last thing the Sergeant needed to hear. She had hoped that a night locked alone in the cells would have shaken Rice up. In the back of her mind, she could still hear the Commissioner's words. If she didn't get some action soon to put a stop to the hospital killings, she and her team would be replaced. Claire wasn't about to throw in the towel just yet. "Leave her in the cells for another night, see if that helps."

"I'm telling you, being in the cells has had no affect on her," Tony stated.

"Maybe not, but with her in the cells at least there's no killing going on. First thing in the morning we'll have another go at her. This time I'll join you."

Chapter 23

Doctor Bevan drove into work with her windows rolled down. This morning, by the time she had woken up, it already had turned warm and sunny outside. A perfect kind of morning for the drive into her office. She didn't mind the short drive back and forth from her condo. At this end of the city, the drive was manageable. Traffic was always light and the speeds were so much more reasonable than the crazy hustle of the inner-city core. At every stop she could hear birds chirping away above the sounds of young kids talking and laughing on their way to school. Today had all the makings of a 'Good Day'.

"Morning Doctor," her assistant Marjorie greeted her. "You seem to be in an awful cheerful mood this morning."

"Who wouldn't be. This is the type of day you'd just like to close up shop and have a picnic out under the trees in the park."

Marjorie sighed at the thought. "That would be nice, but I don't think that's going to happen today."

"What do you mean? The weather's perfect. Our problem 'Angel' is finally locked up in police custody. Things couldn't be better."

"I'd hold on to those thoughts till you've had a chance to read the reports I just placed on your desk. You might just find them interesting."

Marianne shrugged off the ominous comment from her assistant. More than likely Marjorie had gotten herself worked up over nothing, she thought. Today was too nice of a day to take things seriously.

Sitting at her desk, she started to take a quick look over the latest St. Luke's Death Report that she had ordered. A report, she figured, she really should cancel now that Nurse Rice was no longer working. At first glance, the report was just as she expected it would be. The hospital had experienced a normal night. The report indicated a total of nine deaths had occurred in the last 24 hrs.

Reading from the list, she found there were two from a traffic accident as a result of drunk driving. Three were from a failed robbery attempt of one of the city's all-night liquor stores. When she read the next two, she shook her head. What a waste, she thought. Two young teenagers had been rushed into the hospital's emergency department, victims of a Fentanyl overdose. It was the next two deaths that stopped her in her tracks. She hadn't expected to see these. Two senior men, both from the hospital's fourth floor, both with no reason stated for their sudden passing. This can't be right, she thought. She read it again. There was no doubt, the warning flags were clearly there.

Picking up the report she hurried out to her assistant's desk. "Call over to the hospital. I want the bodies from the last two on this list brought over here. Call down to the morgue and tell them to prep for a couple of rush autopsies. And put a call over to Sergeant Reindle. Tell her I need to speak with her right-away. You got that?"

Marjorie had expected that there would be a burst of activity and was prepared to jot everything down as the doctor spouted off the orders. "And what about the picnic? Should I cancel that?" she smirked.

"Don't be smart," Bevan replied. "Nobody likes a smart ass."

Back in her office, disappointed, she slumped down deep into her chair. So much for this being a 'Good Day' she thought.

*****

Inside the interview room the silence was deafening. No one moved a muscle. No one uttered a word. The only sound that could be heard above the low whirl of the ventilation fan was the heavy breathing coming from Detective Swan. Sergeant Reindle, openly stared across the table at Michele. Never a blink. Only the burning stare directly into the eyes of Nurse Rice. The Sergeant knew this was it. Her 72-hour custody time was running out. A lot depended on her forcing Michele to make a mistake. A mistake that could lead to a confession. She had to break this woman.

"Ms. Rice," Claire began in a voice that was strong and carried in it a determination that would not be denied. "I don't know what kind of game you think you are playing at, but I'm going to tell you exactly what's going to happen."

Michele sat politely and listened.

"We have enough evidence to lay a series of First-Degree Murder charges against you. We can directly link you with the deaths of four men at St. Luke's Hospital. The deaths have all occurred over the last two months. The same time period that you began working at the hospital." Claire paused to give the message time to sink into the woman. "Each death occurred during a night shift that you were working as the nurse on the fourth-floor ward. Your plan to throw the orderly, Andrew Brompton, under the bus didn't fool anyone."

"I've told your two henchmen here, and now I'm telling you. I work damn hard at my job and I take the responsibility for the care of my patients seriously," Michele fired back defiantly. She was not going to be bullied by this woman or by anyone. "I feel sorry for the men who have needlessly loss their lives, but it wasn't because of me. I am respected by both the doctors and fellow nurses I work with. Frankly, you and your Detectives are wasting your time trying to blame this on me."

"That's quite an act you have," Claire answered. "You'd do yourself a lot of good if you dropped it. If you confess now, I can promise you it will go a lot easier for you." Claire decided she needed to throw some fear into the woman. "I want to remind you that this state carries the Death Sentence for convicted serial killers. If you confess now, we'll do everything in our power to remove that from the table and get you a sentence of life in prison. ..."

Sergeant Reindle's speech was interrupted in mid threat by a single knock on the door. "I'm sorry to interrupt but ..."

Claire turned and fired back, "Not now!"

Mona knew she had to give her Sergeant the message. "Sergeant, Dr. Bevan is on the phone and she says it's imperative that she talk to you right now."

"Tell her I'll call her back."

"No, she told me to tell you it has to be now."

Claire realized it no longer mattered. The interruption had broken the spell she had been weaving on the nurse. She'd have to start all over from the beginning again.

*****

"What is it?" Claire roared into the phone. "I was right in the middle of interviewing Rice. Another couple of minutes I would have had a confession out of her."

"You'll get no confession out of that woman. She didn't do it!" Although Marianne could tell the Sergeant was wound up and angry with her, she kept an even tone in her voice. She knew Claire wasn't going to like what she had to be told.

"Say that again."

"I'm telling you Nurse Rice isn't the 'Death Angel'."

Claire couldn't believe what she was hearing. "It has to be her. Everything points to her. Even you said it was her. You can't just suddenly decide to change your mind now."

"Calm down and listen to me. I know Nurse Rice is hiding some kind of secret, but she isn't your killer."

"How do you know this?"

"Because last night, while you had Rice locked in your cells, there were two more killings. Both older men, both from the hospital fourth floor. Now granted I haven't done the autopsies yet, but I'm confident these are both 'Angel' killings."

"God Damn It! You know what this means," Claire spoke in pure frustration.

"You're going to have to let Rice go."

"Far more than that," Claire stated. "When the Commissioner hears of this, I'll be the one let go."

"You do know that woman is hiding a secret that she doesn't want anyone to know," Bevan tried to remind the Sergeant.

"You're just as bad as my detectives. Unless her secret has something to do with the murders going on, I don't care about it. The only thing that matters is getting the killer."

Chapter 24

Claire looked around at her apartment. The apartment that only a short time ago had appeared so bright and airy. Now, as she sat on her couch, exhausted, she could feel it's darkness closing in on her. When she had first moved in, a little over a year ago, she had been filled with such hopes and dreams. She had been excited to start in at her new job, Sergeant of Detectives in Homicide. She had visions of the excitement she would have as she worked and solved baffling cases. Visions of how she would rise through the ranks to become a Lieutenant then maybe even a Captain. The events of today had dashed all those dreams away. She didn't know what she was going to do. In all honesty, she thought to herself, she'd like to pack everything up and just move away. Go somewhere new where she could forget everything and start over again, fresh.

Thoughts of her father came tumbling back to her. He had told her whenever she made a mistake, she had to step up and own it. Growth came from learning from your mistakes and to always keep moving forward. But what did he know. He had spent his whole life stuck in a low-level position on the corporate ladder. Always being the one dumped on. He died of bleeding ulcers, brought on by the stress from his struggles and the hardening of his liver that he gave to himself from the drink he needed just to face each day. She took a sip of her warm tea from a mug with '*World's Best Dad*' written on it. She had given it to him one Christmas, as a wide-eyed child, such a long time ago. Drinking her tea, she allowed herself a slight smile. At least she had learned not to try to drink her problems away.

Maybe the Commissioner was right. Maybe she wasn't experienced enough and maybe this case was too complicated for her. She had tried to stay focused on her target. Find the 'Angel' and stop the killings. But it wasn't easy. Her Detective Swan continually wanted to go off chasing Dr. Coleus. Dr. Bevan was fixated with some secret she thought Nurse Rice was hiding. And Detective Morrison, well, he was too damn nice.

Tonight was a night when her mind was filled with doubt about the decisions she had made. In her professional life she had been wrong with the decision she had made about the orderly, Andrew Brompton. She was also proven wrong about the decision she had made about the Nurse Michele Rice. But that wasn't all that filled her mind. Her personal life was a mess. One minute she was madly in love with Jason Alder, then she wasn't, then she was. Her frank talk with Dr.

Bevan had forced her to rethink everything about her feelings towards Jason. She realized Bevan was right. She had let herself become subservient to the needs of Jason. It was on his timetable of when he wanted love regardless of when she needed love. It was only when his wants and desires surfaced that he would turn to her. Restless nights had told her that wasn't how she wanted to live. She felt she wanted, or rather she needed, a love that was bold, filled with the excitement of being together. The excitement of dealing with the ups and downs of life together. But most important, it would have to be a life together as equals. And that kind of life she now had come to know she would never have with Jason.

Finishing her tea, she rose to head for bed and hopefully get some sleep. Tomorrow would be a big day. She would need to be well rested. Tomorrow she would need to face the Commissioner, and tomorrow she would need to face Jason.

*****

"I'm afraid he's not in right now," the Commissioner's Assistant, Nancy, announced. "You can sit over there and wait if you like, he should be back in a couple of minutes." When she looked at the Sergeant, she felt a feeling of concern. "Are you alright?" she asked. "You look exhausted as if you haven't been getting enough sleep."

Before Claire could answer, the Commissioner strode in. When he dropped a stack of papers on Nancy's desk, "File these for me, will ya," he noticed Reindle was sitting, waiting to see him. "Sergeant, come in," he stated. Claire followed him into his office, just as a sheep to the slaughter, she thought.

She took her customary position, standing in front of the oversized desk. "I'm afraid I have some bad news," she started. "We've had to release our suspect who we were holding in connection with the hospital killings."

Baywright already knew that Rice had been released. He had been quietly following the actions of the Sergeant. What he didn't know was 'Why'.

"Go on, explain," he coaxed.

"Nurse Michele Rice gave us every indication that she was the 'Angel' killer. We were confident we had the right person in custody."

"And if you were so confident, as you say you were, what changed?"

Claire swallowed hard. "Unfortunately, while we had her locked in our cells, Dr. Bevan reported that she detected two more sudden deaths had occurred during the night at the hospital."

Baywright sat quietly for a moment. He needed to carefully think through his next actions. "Sergeant, sit down. We need to talk."

Claire had never sat in the Commissioner's office. Normally it was always 'Get in – Get out' as fast as you could. But this time, Claire had a feeling she knew what the Commissioner was about to say.

"Sergeant," he began in his most fatherly voice. "At our last meeting I mentioned that I was concerned that this case was too complicated and you were too inexperienced to handle it. Do you remember that?"

Claire remembered. It was one of the main things she'd been thinking about. "Yes sir."

"And I also mentioned that I had been thinking of removing you as the lead and replacing you with a more experienced officer. Do you remember that?"

Here it comes, she thought. "Yes sir."

As Claire watched the face of the commissioner, she could see he had begun biting his lip. She could tell he was having trouble dealing with the thoughts that were running through his head.

"Sergeant, you've caused me to be doing a lot of thinking. Removing you would be the obvious thing to do, and God knows I should do it." More lip biting and more deep thinking. "But I'm not sure if it would be the right thing to do. If I were to replace everyone of my officers who ran into difficulties attempting to solve a case, I wouldn't have enough personnel to run the department. And it would be doing you a great disservice. How would you ever learn and gain the experience you need if I didn't let you fight your way through your problems."

Claire was trying to process what the Commissioner had said. He wasn't going to replace her after all.

"Sergeant, I can tell you that unknown to you I took the time and met with an old friend of mine. A friend, who over the years, I have learned to value her opinion. I want you to know that Dr. Bevan talked highly of you. She told me of your determination to try to keep everyone, including her, focused on the common goal of finding and putting a stop to the killer."

The more Claire learned about the doctor, the more she realized how terribly wrong she had been about her.

"And Dr. Bevan reminded me that it wasn't all that long ago, when I was a young inexperienced officer, that I needed her help when I was floundering with a tough case."

Claire had noticed the Commissioner's voice had picked up the slightest touch of wistfulness as he spoke.

"I don't have to remind you that people are needlessly being murdered in that hospital and it's up to you to stop it from happening. What I can tell you is you don't have to do it alone."

Claire could feel the fatherly concern coming from Baywright

"Just as I have done on many occasions, you need to draw on Dr. Bevan for help. Learn to trust her and to use her experience along with your determination to solve this case. And to help remove one of the distractions that you have had, I've ordered the Organized Crime Group to move forward against this Dr. Coleus and that racketeer Logan.

*****

As soon as Michele had been released from police custody, there were two things she needed to do. The first, she had to rush home to her apartment and feed her cats. She knew being away for one day or even two was okay, but for the cats to be left on their own for going on three days, now that was pushing it. The second was she needed to meet with Doris Hopkins.

"Can I help you?" the little pixie that Doris had for a receptionist asked.

"Can you tell Ms. Hopkins that Michele Rice is here and would like to see her?"

No sooner had the girl relayed the message, than the inner office door burst open and Doris literally flew out to greet Michele. Her outstretched arms wrapped Michele in a hug tight enough that Michele had no choice but to hold her breath.

"My dear, my dear," Doris bubbled. "Are you alright? Did they hurt you?" She released the hug and took a step back. "Here, let me have a look at you, you poor thing. I'm so glad you're okay. Come into my office, you look tired." Doris turned to her receptionist, "I don't want to be disturbed."

With Michele safely settled into one of the office chairs, Doris was beside herself. She couldn't contain her excitement. She couldn't sit, she could barely talk. She flittered around almost giggling out loud.

Michele was amazed at this display from Doris. She was aware that the woman had a fondness for her, Michele had already used that to her advantage. But this, this was way over the top. Michele had worked out what she wanted and how she was going to get it. She'd start off playing for sympathy. Then once Doris was onboard, she'd switch to a '*Please sir. Can I have some more*' approach.

"I'm terribly sorry I missed working my last three-night shifts. There was nothing I could do. They locked me up in a cell and wouldn't let me talk with anyone. I wanted to tell you I couldn't be at work so you wouldn't worry about me, but I just couldn't."

Doris was filled with empathy for the suffering that she believed Michele had been forced to endure. "I know, I know. It wasn't your fault. I couldn't believe that anyone could possibly think you were capable of doing those terrible things."

"They questioned me and questioned me for hours. I was so exhausted, but they wouldn't stop." Michele, with her lies, was laying it on thick for the gullible Doris.

Doris had moved behind Michele and had begun to stroke the woman's hair as if she was a cat.

"I know it's a lot to ask," Michele hesitated.

"What, what? Ask me anything."

"It's just that I'm so tired and with the emotional stress I've been under, I'm afraid I'm not thinking straight."

"I understand."

"I'm worried in my condition I might do something wrong with one of my patients. If I make a mistake and give the wrong medicine to someone, they'd think I did it on purpose."

"No, no, we can't have that."

"Do you think I could have a couple more days off so I can rest and try to pull myself back together?" After the display Doris had put on, Michele didn't want to tell her the real reason she needed the time off. She needed the time to move into her new house with Andrew.

"Yes, of course you can."

When Michele went to leave the office, it dawned on her that something was missing. "You're missing one of your lovely cat pictures."

"I know. There was an unfortunate accident and it got broken."

*****

"Claire," Jason pleaded. "We can't keep doing this." He stood in the doorway to her apartment in a vain attempt to sway her. An hour ago, she had phoned him and told him of her decision to end their relationship, this time for good. But he wasn't ready to accept that it was over between them. Throwing his phone down, he had rushed over to talk face to face with her. It had taken a long time for him to finally come to grips with the notion that he, of all people, could possibly be in love. He knew, in the past, he had made mistakes in dealing with Claire's feelings. Mistakes he now regretted. He had apologized to her. He had explained his initial hesitation to being in a committed relationship. He had thought there was far too much life to live and explore before he could see himself tied down to just one woman. But that was before he had come to realize that Claire wasn't just an ordinary woman. He didn't know how it happened, but she had slipped inside of his conscience and had become an overwhelming part of him. He couldn't help himself. He couldn't stop thinking about her. Everyday she was in his thoughts.

As hard as it was for her, Claire realized she had no choice. She loved this man, but she wasn't prepared to give up on her dreams of finding the perfect man. A man who fully loved and respected her for who she was. Her talk with Bevan opened her eyes. She now knew that a man like Jason would never be happy with surrendering himself to one woman. Bevan had convinced her that while a relationship with Jason might start off all wonderful and rosy, it wouldn't take long before he would grow to resent her for tying him down.

"I've told you it's over between us. No amount of talking or promises will make me change my mind. What we had was good, but it just isn't enough for me. Dr. Bevan helped me face what I had been struggling to avoid."

At the sound of Marianne's name, Jason exploded. "Why the hell would you be listening to her? She has no business standing between us. You have to see that she has some sort of sick fantasy. Don't let her do this to us."

Claire began to close her door, "I'm sorry. Dr. Bevan told me the truth and I believe her. It's over."

From the other side of the closed door, Jason didn't know if he should cry or if he should be angry. But he did know he'd had enough of his boss, Bevan.

*****

"You think you're so bloody smart, don't you. You couldn't just leave us alone. You had to stick you're nose in and spoil everything." Jason had barged into his boss's office, fuming.

He towered over her as she sat at her desk, uncertain as to why he was so violently verbally abusing her. His face had turned scarlet red, his eyes tore into her as the bulged veins in his neck pulsed rapidly. Had it been anyone other than Jason, she would have been afraid. Seeing the distressed state he was in worried her. She felt she needed to try to calm him down before he injured himself. In a soothing voice, "Jason, you need to calm down. I don't know what's got you so riled up, but I can't help you until you calm down."

"Don't you understand? I don't want your help. It's your help that has ruined everything."

Marianne knew there was only one thing that could make a man go this crazy. A woman. "Has something happened between you and that Police Sergeant?"

"As if you didn't know. Don't try to act so innocent, you're not fooling me. Claire told me what you said to her. You told her to dump me because you were jealous that we loved each other and that you were the one who would be left all alone, on your own."

So, she finally did it, Bevan thought. The Sergeant had taken her advice and stood up for herself. Well good for her. But now she had to deal with the messy aftermath. "Jason, right now you're not thinking straight. In your heart you know that Claire made the right decision. The two of you would have learned to hate each other if you stayed together."

"But that decision was up to us to discover, not you. You stole any chance of finding happiness away from us. You had no right. I'm looking at the only one I hate and it's you."

"Jason, I know you're upset right now, but when you come to your senses, you'll thank me," the Doctor said, trying to reassure him that everything will work out for the better. "I want you to take some time off, take a week. Use that time to pull yourself together so we can get back to work."

"I don't need any time off. As of now I resign. I can't work for someone I no longer have any respect for. You'll have my resignation on your desk before the end of the day," he stated as he turned to leave. "And I never, ever want to be associated with you again."

Marianne never said anything. When she received the resignation letter, she'd just hold it in her desk. After awhile, when he cools down and has time to think, he'll be back, she thought.

Chapter 25

Promptly at ten o'clock, George Logan stepped from the elevator into the hospital's dimly lit corridor. Wearing no suit, no white shirt, or tie, he looked for all the world as if he might have been one of the hospital's night janitors. With his plaid short sleeved shirt, khaki slacks and a pair of loafers, he wasn't dressed to impress. There was no one in the hospital that he needed to impress. He knew he had Coleus right where he wanted him, and in a short while, Coleus would also know it. From the open office door, he could see the light burning in the inner office.

George crossed through the outer office with his hand out in greeting, "Dr. Coleus?"

The Doctor sat behind his desk and never moved to accept the greeting. "You've got a lot of nerve barging in here. Who the hell are you?" Mark had been just at the point of wrapping things up for the day so he could finally go home. He was tired, worn out and in no mood to waste any time this late at night on some stranger. "If you want to see me, make an appointment during normal business hours. I don't talk with strangers who wander into my office, unannounced, this late at night. So I'd advise you to just turn around and leave before I call security and have you forcibly removed."

Logan just grinned as he thought to himself, *'This pompous ass is going to be taught a real lesson. A lesson he's not easily going to forget.'* "I did this for your benefit, not mine," George replied. "I thought you'd appreciate us meeting privately out of the eyesight of the people here until we get our relationship established."

Coleus wanted to make it clear, "We have no relationship. I don't know who you are and I don't care to know." During the course of his career, the doctor, had never been confronted by anyone in the criminal world and the mere presence of this man intimidated him.

Logan stared at Coleus for what seemed like hours to the doctor but was in fact only a brief minute. "Now Mark. You don't mind if I call you Mark, do you?" George said setting the tone of the conversation. "We do know each other. In fact, I'd say we know each other rather well. You and your lovely wife, Alex, have been acquaintances of mine for quite sometime now." George could see that the doctor was confused. "To start off with, you need to understand, to me, this is business. Just business. You don't have to like me, that's not what's important. What is important is that between us we have an understanding." Logan wanted to make sure he cut through the doctor's defences.

"What in the world are you talking about?" Coleus asked. This man had to be crazy. He had never seen him before in his life, and there was no way his wife Alex could possibly know who he was. Mark started to lift his phone to call for security.

"I don't think you'll want to be calling anybody just yet," Logan said with a voice carrying the unmistakable sound of a threat. "You need to realize all those so-called business trips you've been on and the kickbacks you've been taking from your hospital expansion contracts, come from me."

When he heard that piece of information, Coleus was shocked. His wife, Alex, had convinced him the gifts he had been receiving were all part of good business. "I don't understand," he mumbled. "Everything I was given was in appreciation from the contracting companies."

"Don't be so stupid," Logan laughed. "I own those companies. And those gifts of all that money you've been raking in, are called '*Kick Backs*' and could get you locked up for five to ten years."

"You don't mean this. I'll go to the police; tell them it was all just a mistake. They'll believe me and my wife. After all, you're the criminal, not us."

Logan shook his head. "You dumb fool! Your wife has a serious problem. You've left her alone for far too long and she's started going out looking to have some fun. And once wives develop a taste for fun, it's a taste that you're not going to be able to stop by trying to lock her away in that house of yours. She's stumbled into the high-flying party scene and has become a frequent visitor to a number of the night clubs I control. You know Alex is an attractive woman," he paused to make sure Coleus understood exactly what he was saying. "She could be a real asset to my organization. I want you to think, how long would it take before I have complete control of your wife? She's already sampling some of the party favors my people have been giving her. You need to think hard because you've got a decision to make."

Mark was stunned by the ease with which Logan talked about dominating Alex's future. He had been worried about the intimidating threats and possible violence against himself that this man was showing he was capable of. He hadn't really thought about his wife. Did she deserve to suffer because of what he had done? Was his ego that big and that strong that he could sacrifice her? He stared at Logan, taking stock of the man. The coldness that radiated from George sent a shiver though him. He didn't like it, but he had no choice. He had to make a deal with this devil. "What is it you want?"

George smiled as he stretched out in one of the doctor's chairs. "That's better. Now that we understand each other, let's get down to business so you can get out of here and go home to your lovely wife," George jabbed, just to rub salt in the doctor's face.

Reaching into his pocket he pulled out a small USB thumb drive. "Put this in your computer. There's a short video I want you to see."

Mark did what he was told. His computer screen flickered for a moment before becoming clear. On his screen he watched a group of young men, pinning a younger boy down on a couch. The scene looked like it was a college type frat boy hazing. As three of the young men held the boy down, the fourth young man was forcibly pouring a large bottle of liquor down the held boy's throat. As the younger boy struggled, gasped, gagged for air, the four paid no heed, but only laughed at the innocent boy.

"You see the tall one pouring the liquor down the boy's throat? Do you recognize him?" George asked the doctor.

Mark stared at the terrible event on his screen.

"That, my friend, is the future mayor of this city, Ruger Shultz. The younger boy unfortunately died from alcohol poisoning. Shultz's father, being rich and powerful, paid off the other boys' parents handsomely to keep his son out of the investigation."

Mark was appalled at the thought of his recent friend being one of the prime instigators of this horrible scene. How was Ruger Shultz allowed to escape justice and later take up the honored position of Mayor of the City? Coleus couldn't believe what he had just watched. "How … Where did you get this video?" he stammered. "And why on earth are you showing it to me?"

"The how and where I got this video isn't important for you to know. It's the why that's important. I have it on good authority that the Organized Crime Group is going to be coming for me," George replied. "Shortly, I'm going to be arrested on a number of criminal charges. It doesn't matter if these charges are true or not, because this video is my 'Get Out of Jail Card'.

Mark didn't grasp the meaning of what this criminal was telling him. "This video is horrible, but how could it possibly help you?"

George now told the confused doctor, "You travel in some pretty sophisticated circles. I want you to get word to our illustrious mayor that you have this video. Let him know, that unless he calls off the dogs who are chasing me, this video will be sent to every TV news station in existence. When people see it, Ruger Shultz, won't be able to run for dog catcher any where in the country."

"You want me to blackmail the mayor of this city for you?" Mark said in astonishment.

"No, I want you to blackmail the mayor for your wife," a smiling George replied. "You can either do as you're told, and everything will be alright. Alex will find herself barred from any club in the area. Or I'll be sending you pictures of your wife, working for me as you rot away in prison. The choice is yours."

As Logan got up from his seat and began to leave, "I suggest you lock that USB drive somewhere safe. Neither of us would want to have anything happen to it."

*****

Mark Coleus stormed into his house and headed directly to the den to find his wife, Alex, who was leisurely lounging on the settee, talking on her phone.

"Hang up," he commanded.

Alex was surprised to see her husband home so early. With her phone still held tightly to her ear, "I'm talking with my sister." She lied, and hoped her husband didn't hear the real voice on the other end of her phone.

"I don't care who you're talking to. I said, hang up."

Alex ended her phone conversation, "That was rude."

Mark glared down on his wife. She was the reason he was now drawing attention from both the police and the Medical Examiner's Office. And now, because of her, he was being forced into becoming the worst kind of criminal there is, a blackmailer! All during the drive home he tried to figure out what he was going to say to her. With every thought of his wife, he got angrier and angrier.

These last couple of months, he had been continually working late on the new hospital wing designs. With her husband never home, Alex, his wife had become increasingly bored from being couped up alone in their empty house. At the time, Mark was fairly certain that while he was working hard, she was safely home, doing the things that housewives normally do. It never dawned on him that she would be out running around. His wife didn't do those types of things.

He had known that she was bored. She had complained to him often enough. He had ignored it. He couldn't let himself get bogged down with the goings on of a bored housewife. He had to stay focused on the hospital expansion. It was too important to him. The 'Mark Coleus Wing' was a legacy that would live on for years and years to come. He had even started to put extra money in her household budget, when she had asked him, thinking that would satisfy her, but it didn't. She continued to demand more and more money. It was her who had convinced him that if Contractors and Developers wanted to give away money and gifts, he'd be a fool not to take it. A touch of uncertainty flashed across his mind. How in the world could he explain to her that the money she was using for this fast life she was now living had put him in criminal jeopardy?

"I had a surprising visit this evening from someone who claimed to be a friend of yours, a George Logan."

"So?" Alex scoffed.

"Is that all you've got to say, 'So'?"

"What do you want me to say?" She was happily spending his money on her night time adventures. "You're never home. I'm trapped in this mausoleum by myself. I've made some new friends who think I'm fun to be around."

Now he knew for certain it was true, Mark thought to himself. Everything that crook Logan had told him was true. All this time while he was working hard, trying to make things better for both of them, trying to become more than just a doctor, trying to become a 'Somebody', Alex had been busily running around. And it wasn't bad enough that she was running around, she was involved with the most intimidating man he had ever had the misfortune to meet.

"You little fool. These friends of yours are only around you because you're spending money like water on them. These people aren't your friends. They're piranha who chew up stupid people like you every day. And worst of all, you're spending money that we don't have and now it's jeopardizing both my career and my hospital expansion."

"Your hospital expansion, that's all you care about. I'm sick of it," Alex said, striking back at her husband. "This isn't my fault. It's your fault. If you showed me any kind of attention, showed me you loved me, or at least cared for me instead of that damn hospital of yours'."

Mark waved his arms around, exposing the spacious house. "I did all this for you. I've been working night and day trying to give you everything a woman could want."

"You haven't been working for me," she screamed back at him. "You've been working to feed your own ego," Alex answered as her eyes swelled up with tears. "You've gotten yourself into this mess by trying to be a big man. Well now it looks like you're going to have to pay for it."

Mark slumped down into a chair. It was pointless trying to talk with his wife. She had no concept of the trouble he was facing. His future ahead consisted of possible criminal charges if the police found out about the contract kick backs, he had been taking. Then there was the threat of suspension of his doctor's licence for the fraudulent medical claims he had been filing. And on top of all this, there was a serial killer running wild in his hospital. He had to do something quick. It was all falling apart. He decided that in the morning he'd have to do what Logan wanted. He'd have to blackmail his friend, the mayor.

*****

The gray day that surrounded him did nothing to cheer up the Doctor as he approached the front gates to the Mayor's Mansion. It only helped to add to the somber mood that he was already in. When he had left his home this morning, his wife Alex was still asleep in her bed. The fight they had last night resulted in him having to sleep in his den. His back ached. He was wearing the same clothes as he had worn yesterday. All his clean clothes were still hanging in his closet in the bedroom, but Alex had refused to let him in. He was unshaven, unwashed and worse of all, he smelled and he knew it.

On all his past visits to the mansion, the gates would automatically open for him. Then with a casual wave to the security guard he would drive right up to the front steps. Today, for some reason, it was different. As he approached the black iron gates, they never moved. He could see the security guard standing in his guard shack, but the guard made no attempt to open the gates. In frustration he honked his horn. No movement. He honked it again. Still no movement. Was the bloody man deaf? This time he leaned on the horn. The loud blare startled a couple of birds that had nested in the decorative bushes that surrounded the front of the property.

"Can I help you sir?" the guard asked sarcastically when he finally came out of his shack.

“Of course, you can help me. What do you think I’m out here blasting my horn for?”

The guard was unfazed by the Doctor’s outburst. “Sir, this is the Mayor’s Mansion and it is not open for visitors. Unless you have an appointment, I’m going to have to ask you to leave.”

Coleus was getting madder and madder having to deal with this fool. “I know this is the Mayor’s Mansion. Ruger Shultz is a personal friend of mine. I’ve been here several times in the past and have never been treated like this before.”

“If you’ll give me your name, I’ll see if anyone is expecting you.”

Coleus gave his name and waited. He could see the guard on the phone talking to someone.

“Alright sir,” the guard said. “If you’ll just pull up to the side there, Mrs. Shultz will see you.” He pointed to a slim uniformed guard sitting in a golf cart beside the parking area. “The guard there will escort you to the back garden.”

As soon as he parked his car, the slim guard motioned for the Doctor to get in the golf cart. “Hang on,” he said as the cart zipped around to the back of the building.

"Grace, what's going on? These idiots treated me as if I was some kind of a stranger," he complained to the mayor's wife.

Grace looked at the doctor and grimaced, "You look like hell."

"I've had a long night at the hospital," he lied. "I've come because I need your help."

Grace's face was cold. She showed no compassion for the sorry sight before her. In a calm, clear voice, a voice devoid of any emotion, she started, "I'm meeting you outside here because I don't want anyone in the mansion to see me talking with you. You are no longer welcome to come here and attempt to bother the mayor. Do I make myself clear?"

Coleus was stunned by the coldness of the order. "You better hear what I have to say before you start making any demands," Coleus snapped back.

Grace was prepared for this. She had to make the cut with force if necessary. "Let me make it so you understand. I've received inside information that the Organized Crime Squad have you linked into an investigation involving George Logan. Why in the world would you allow yourself to be associated with the number one Racketeer and Drug Lord in this state? He owns the 'Franco Construction & Engineering Company'. Does any of this ring a bell with you?"

Of course, the doctor knew of the Franco Company. They were the lead contractors on his hospital expansion project and had been more than generous with various favors to him before he had known anything about any criminal ties with Logan.

"I've been told," Grace continued. "That when your bank accounts were examined, they found evidence that you've been receiving substantial amounts of kickbacks from Logan. Kickbacks using money that they have been able to trace to 'Public Funds' for God's sake. You are one step away from spending five to ten years in prison."

Coleus felt he needed to defend himself. It was one thing for a criminal like George Logan to attack him, but he wasn't going to take any abuse from Grace. "I only received a few gifts. My wife, Alex, told me it was how big business was done," he tried to claim in his defence. "At the time, I had no idea of any links to Logan."

She couldn't believe that one man could be so stupid. She gave a sarcastic laugh. "Your wife Alex told you, did she? Did she also tell you that she's been spotted by surveillance as being a late-night companion of Logan?"

Coleus could take no more. His body began to tremble. There were no secrets. Apparently, everyone except him had known of his wife's indiscretions. He could hold back no longer. This pushy woman needed to be put in her place.

"Grace," he started with his eyes locked on to the laughing woman. "No matter what I mistakenly might have done and no matter what personal problems I have with my wife, they are nothing compared to the problem you now have!"

The laughter stopped. Grace had enough political experience to recognize a threat when she heard one. "What do you mean, problem that I have?"

Mark went on in great detail, to describe the horrendous video that Logan had given him. "It's not so funny now, is it?" he jabbed. He was enjoying this. For far too long it had been him who was at the centre of problems. As he looked at the mayor's wife, he knew he had hit his mark. He watched as the blood drained from her face and her eyes turned to moon sized saucers.

Grace erupted into a full-blown panic attack. "Get him out of here!" she ordered to the security guard. "Get him out of here now!" she screamed. "If I ever see him in here again, you and your whole group will be looking for new jobs."

"Yes maam," the guard said as he hurriedly slipped an arm around the doctor and pulled him towards the golf cart. "Right away maam."

"This isn't the end of this, Grace. You're making a terrible mistake for your husband," Coleus yelled back as he was being forcibly dragged away.

Chapter 26

Michele sat by herself, in the sunroom, with her feet lazily resting on the footstool while she gazed out the window. Beside her, a hot cup of tea had been placed on a coaster by Andrew. She had learned it was easy to train Andrew to respond to her needs, he was so eager to please her. Curled up on the settee, enjoying the warmth of the afternoon sun, her two cats had made themselves at home.

Cleaning the house, from top to bottom had proven to be a daunting task. She kept Andrew working non-stop throughout the days and long into the nights. He swept, vacuumed, washed, scrubbed until every room sparkled. He never complained, always smiled and asked what did she want him to do next. To him it wasn't work, it was a game that he played with his friend, Nurse Rice. In the evenings, when they stopped for dinner, they always toasted with sweet red wine, using his mother's crystal glass ware. Michele had no intention to repeat the mistake she made of drinking wine out of oversized water tumblers as she had done with her last toasts with Andrew.

"Andrew," she called out. "Have you finished washing this morning's dishes yet? We won't be able to have dinner until all your chores are done." She could hear him scurrying around in the kitchen. Dishes were rattling, cupboard doors were opening and closing. Michele was quite happy with herself. In a very short period of time, she had turned Andrew's house from one of chaos into an organized, clean home for her and her cats.

The outside of the house was another matter. From the street, passers by were unaware of the changes within. The weeds still grew rampant in the flower garden, the grass still grew wild and the large black garbage bags still filled the outside porch. Michele didn't want to draw any unwanted attention to her new home. The less nosey people knew the better, she thought.

She heard a knock. Then another one. Then another one. Someone, knocking on the front door was insistent that the door be answered. Michele sat quietly. She wasn't expecting anyone since she had told no one of her move. When she left her apartment, she took with her only a few of her personal affects, her clothes and her cats. The rest she deemed as of having no value so she left them. Someone else could have the pleasure of throwing her old, cat damaged couch, out for the trash. Her new house had everything she needed and more.

The knocking noise disturbed the cats. Roused from their sleep, they jumped down and headed towards the door, curious as to what the noise was about. Michele made a lunge to try to grab the cats but they were too fast for her.

"Ms. Hopkins," she heard Andrew say. He had answered the door. She had warned him to never answer the door unless she told him to. Later she'd have to have words with him, but right now, she had to deal with this intruder. Doris Hopkins was the last person she wanted to see. She wasn't ready to deal with Doris and this could get messy.

With the door open, Doris could see the cats. From their description she knew who they belonged to. "Andrew, is Nurse Rice here with you? Those are her cats, aren't they?"

Andrew didn't know what to do. Not only had Nurse Rice told him to never answer the door, but she had also told him to never tell anyone that she now lived with him.

"It's alright Andrew," Michele stated. "You can go back to doing your chores. I'll take care of Ms. Hopkins."

Relieved to be off the hot seat, Andrew quickly retreated back to the kitchen.

"Doris, what brings you here?"

Still standing in the doorway, "Aren't you going to invite me in?" Doris asked hopefully.

"Well, I wasn't expecting any visitors, but come in. We can sit in the sunroom."

In the sunroom Doris looked around. "This seems awful cozy."

Michele could tell by the tone in Doris's voice that she was being sarcastic.

Doris was a little annoyed with what she saw and a little concerned that her friend was involved with Andrew of all people. Everyone in the hospital knew of Andrew's situation. It was no secret that he was, as the nurses say, 'A little below standard'. "I was worried about you and wanted to check to see that you were ok."

"That's so sweet of you," Michele cooed.

"I went to your apartment and they told me you had moved out," Doris continued. "It was only when I found out Andrew had been missing from work that I put two and two together. When you told me you needed some time off to pull yourself together from your police ordeal, I never expected that you were lying to me. I thought we were friends. Didn't I tell you to take as much time as you needed? You didn't have to do this. If you needed a place to stay, you could have stayed with me."

Michele needed to turn this around. Now that her life was beginning to take shape, she had to be careful not to upset Doris. At work in the hospital, she didn't want to constantly have to be watching her back for whatever mood Doris was in. "It's not what you think. I'm not here because I want to be," she lied. "Andrew came to me and told me he too was in trouble with the police." She was telling a half truth because it suited her. "He told me that the police were going to place him in a care facility. What could I do? I'm only here to help him. He's such a lost soul."

Doris listened to what Michele was telling her. It made sense, but she didn't like it. She was filled with a growing feeling of jealousy. She finally had a friend. A friend she cared about, worried about, and had even threatened the Medical Examiner to get her freed from police custody. And now her friend was abandoning her to help a man.

Michele knew of Doris's feelings towards men. "It's good to have a man wait on you for a change. Here let me get something for you. Andrew," she yelled out. "Bring some tea in here for my guest."

Doris liked this. Maybe she was wrong. This is how it should be. This is how her lazy husband should have waited on her. "Are you coming back to work?"

"Yes, of course. I remember you once saying, '*Us cat people have to stick together*'." Michele, happy that she had done it again, replied with a huge smile on her face.

Chapter 27

In the early morning darkness, Mark drove his car through the torrential downpour of rain that steadily beat against his windshield. His mood was so low, he barely realized it was raining. Even though he didn't feel like it, he had to force himself to go to work. What was the point he thought. Everything was going wrong. His wife hated him and made him spend his nights alone, sleeping in his den. Dr. Bevan was threatening to take him before the State Medical Board for falsifying official Medical Records for his own gain. The Police Organized Crime Group was on the verge of charging him with Racketeering, and a major crime boss was forcing him to blackmail his only friend.

The only bright light he had left in his life, was his hospital's new expansion wing. And now, on top of all his other problems, construction on the 'Mark Coleus Wing' appeared to be falling behind schedule. He didn't know if the construction slowdown was another one of Logan's tactics to apply added pressure on to him. He only hoped he could hold on long enough to see it through to completion.

He remembered it had been a glorious affair when dignitaries came from all over to be part of the initial Ground Breaking Ceremony. Considering all that was going on, when the wing would be finally completed, he wondered how many of them would shy away when it came time for the official Ribbon Cutting Ceremony. And, when all his failures became known to the public, would the hospital board still place his name on the facility, or would some faceless bureaucrat who did nothing to earn it, now receive that honor? It was only pure willpower, driven by the force of his ego, that kept him moving forward.

Today he had decided to inspect the hospital work site for himself before any of the workers showed up. He wanted to see first hand what the real status of the construction was.

*****

Sergeant Reindle struggled to get out of bed. Ever since her breakup with Jason, she rarely slept. In her mind she knew the breakup was the right thing to do, but she was having a hard time convincing her heart. An early morning call from Dr. Bevan told her she urgently needed to meet her at the hospital.

Bevan, alone, without her investigator by her side, had spent most of the night pouring over the medical records of the 'Angel' deaths. She went over and over them, looking for what she knew had to be there. Somewhere in this mass of paper it was hidden and she was determined that she wouldn't stop hunting until it revealed itself to her. After hours of reading, with bleary eyes and dry parched lips, she had almost quit. She didn't know how much more she could do. Self doubt had begun to creep in to cloud her brain. Maybe she was too old to be doing this anymore. Maybe she should have retired, stepped out of the way to let the younger minds of Sergeant Reindle and Jason do the work that she no longer could do. In one last desperate push she found it. And like most elusive searches, once the answer was exposed, it all appeared to be so simple. She knew who the 'Death Angel' was. It was staring her in the face the whole time but she was either too stupid or too pigheaded to see it.

Now, with Sergeant Reindle, she had to race to the hospital in the hope of stopping one last killing that she knew was coming this morning.

*****

The construction site was a mud bath from the torrential rain that had poured down across the city all night long. Although he had been receiving weekly status reports of the new wing's progress, what he had observed, when he looked out of his office window, didn't appear to match up with what he was being told. The reports only highlighted the successful tasks that had been completed and never mentioned anything about the areas that had fallen behind schedule. Without the morning sun being up, his inspection proved to be foolish. He really couldn't see anything and all he had managed to do was to cover his polished shoes and pant cuffs with a solid coating of thick, sticky brown mud.

When he finally admitted his mistake to himself, he entered the side stairwell of the hospital. Stamping his feet, he tried unsuccessfully to knock off some of the mud, but it was too thick and stubbornly clung to the shoes. Ruined for nothing, he thought to himself. Now he was going to have to throw them away.

He rarely took the elevators. He hated being squeezed inside with a group of hospital visitors. Invariably someone would recognize him and would take the opportunity, while he was trapped, unable to escape, to bombard him with questions. ' … How's my aunt, I don't think she looks very good this morning … I've been having a pain, right here, on my shoulder. Do you think it's something I should be worried about? … What's the real deal about eating Red Meat? My wife says I can't eat steak anymore …' And besides, being a Cardiac Doctor, he knew taking the steps was far better for him then riding in an elevator.

The stairwell was dimly lit. He had complained to the maintenance department several times in the past that they needed to improve the lighting. It was damn well unsafe and it didn't help that the mud on his shoes made the stairs slippery. Travelling up from the ground floor he passed the first floor, then the second.

On the third floor landing he lost his footing and scraped his knee on the edge of one of the concrete steps. '*Damn it!*' his pants now had a tear in them, right through one of the legs. It wasn't his morning.

As he approached the fourth-floor landing, he got the feeling he wasn't alone. Looking up he noticed a shadowy figure had stepped back into the darkness in an attempt not to be seen.

"Who's there?"

No answer.

"Come on, I know you're there. What are you doing?"

No answer.

Getting angry, he rushed up the last couple of steps to confront the intruder.

"Doris, is that you? Why didn't you answer me?"

Still no answer.

"Stop playing games. I've got no time for this," he demanded. In the dim light he was sure it was Doris Hopkins, but her face didn't look quite right to him. It was locked hard. Her eyes were fixed wide open. He could hear her labored breathing, but she refused to speak. In her hand she was holding something. What was it? A syringe. She was holding a hypodermic syringe!

He pointed, "Why have you got that? What is it you think you're doing?"

Finally, she spoke, in a calm monotone voice, showing no sign of emotion. "I'm doing my work. There's so much still to be done."

Coleus was confused. He didn't understand anything that was going on and was fast losing his temper. "What in the world do you mean, '*you're doing your work*'? You should be in your office. Stop this foolishness right now," he demanded.

"The men. The men keep bothering my nurses. They're fat, lazy, laying in bed, constantly bothering my nurses. I have to stop them. They need to be stopped."

Suddenly it hit him. He put it all together. "It's you! You're the 'Angel'. It's been you all along." He had to do something, but what. This 'Angel' had caused him nothing but problems, and now he had a chance to make it right. If he could stop Doris the authorities would see him as a hero. They would stop the vendetta they had on him. "Doris, I'm here to help you. You don't really want to be doing this." He slowly reached out, "Here, give me the needle. It's alright, just give me the needle then we can talk. Everything will be alright. I promise," he coached with his voice staying as sweet as he could hold it.

When Doris heard the '*I promise*' it sparked her. "You men, you're all the same. You promise everything, but you're nothing but mean vicious liars." In one swift movement she moved directly in front of the doctor, face to face, and with no warning she kicked him. Kicked him hard. '*Whomp*'. The Doctor doubled over in tremendous pain and groaned. But Doris wasn't done yet. A second kick forced the doctor backwards and he fell, crashing down the concrete stairs. Legs flailing, arms waving, down he went. Past the third floor, unable to stop. Past the second floor, gaining speed, steadily downward.

Crash! Thump! Bang! He hit into Nurse Berna. In a gesture to make up for arriving late yesterday, when her car wouldn't start, Berna had come into work early to relieve Michele. She had recently started herself on a health kick and had begun taking the stairs. When the hurling body of Coleus struck her, it knocked her legs out from under her and threw her flying, up into the air, until she landed with a '*Thud*' on top of the doctor and rode him, like a toboggan, all the way down to the bottom of the staircase. Coleus came to a stop with a loud '*Crack*' as his head hit the concrete. By the time Nurse Berna had regained her senses, she felt her hand resting in a warm pool of dark, sticky fluid that had seeped from the back of the dead Doctor's head.

*****

"Doris, you're in awful early," Michele greeted the woman as Doris entered the ward from the stairwell.

"I'm just finishing up my night shift report. Berna promised she'd be in early to relieve me this morning."

Doris appeared calm and rested. On the outside, she had fully recovered from her dazed state that had only moments ago taken control of her. Her right hand, still holding the loaded syringe, hung loosely at her side. Michele noticed the needle and thought it queer for Doris to be carrying it around.

"Doris," Michele asked. "Why are you carrying around that needle? Did someone leave it somewhere?"

Doris looked down at her hand and appeared surprised that she was still holding her weapon. "No, I need it for the work I'm doing," she answered in a calm matter of fact voice.

Michele knew something wasn't right. There was no 'Work' that the Director of Nursing would be doing that required her to be carrying around a loaded syringe. "Doris, are you alright?" Then thinking she added, "Maybe you should give me that needle and I'll put it away for you."

Doris never took her eyes off of the syringe. "No, it's important I finish my work."

Michele was now starting to get really worried. Although outwardly, Doris appeared calm and rested, inwardly, Michele sensed that she had lost touch with reality. "What work do you need to do that requires you to use a syringe?"

"You know. I've been doing it all for you. Then you turned on me. You chose Andrew instead of me."

Doris had now begun to scare Michele. "What have you been doing for me? What do you mean, I've chosen Andrew? You're not making any sense."

"It's a secret. I haven't told anyone about your secret, so now I have to make sure you don't tell anyone about mine. We were just like two sisters who shared secrets together, until you changed," the woman giggled.

When Michele heard Doris say that she knew of her secret, the hairs on the back of her neck stood up. "What secret of mine do you think you know?"

"I contacted my friend in Pittsburgh where you used to work. She told me your husband didn't leave you as you've been telling everyone. He died suddenly of a massive heart attack. A heart attack that was labelled as suspicious. I know you killed him! Just like I've been killing all these worthless men who have been bothering you while you tried to work."

Michele turned cold and her body stiffened. It all fell into place. She was looking at the 'Death Angel'. The killer that the police had been hounding her about. She had to do something. Slowly she moved over directly in front of the woman. With a comforting smile on her face, she reached down and gently took the syringe out of Doris's hand. Then, with one quick move, she drove it deep into Doris's neck.

Doris's eyes popped open in surprise. "Why," was all she could say as she crumpled to the floor.

Michele, with ice in her veins answered, "Because some secrets have to remain secret!"

From the corner of her eye, Michele noticed Andrew had been standing near by and had watched the whole scenario play out. "Andrew," she spoke firmly. "The police are going to come and I need you to help me."

Andrew never said anything.

"When they ask you, you are to say that Ms. Hopkins attacked me and in the scuffle the needle got stuck in her neck. Do you understand that? I need for you to tell them it was self defence. Will you do that for me?"

Andrew was frozen. He wanted to help Nurse Rice; she was so good to him. He had heard the women talking. He knew their secrets. He saw Nurse Rice, stab Ms. Hopkins with the needle. He wanted to help Nurse Rice, but in his head, he could hear the voice of his mother telling him '*Good boys always tell the truth*'. And he always did what his mother said.

Fini

Manufactured by Amazon.ca
Bolton, ON

37566301R00173